D0840653

# Why People Do What They Do

## By

# Emilio Iasiello

W & B Publishers
USA

W & B Publishers

For information:
W & B Publishers
9001 Ridge Hill Street
Kernersville, NC 27284

www.a-argusbooks.com

ISBN: 9781635540130

This is a work of *fiction.* All of the characters, organizations and events portrayed in this novel are either products of the author's imagination or used fictitiously.

Book Cover designed by Dubya

Printed in the United States of America

## Dedication

This book is dedicated to my wife, Carmen, beautiful daughter, Elisabetta, and my son, Mimmuccio, who are now, and will always be, my inspiration.

## Acknowledgements

A great debt of gratitude is owed to my agent, Jeanie Loiacono, who took a chance on an unknown writer, to Aurelia Sands and Karen Lock whose tireless efforts and professionalism were very much appreciated, and to William Connor for his invaluable commitment and contribution to the written word.

I'd also like to thank Stephen Goodwin and my professors at George Mason University for being tough but fair evaluators of creative writing. I can't imagine a more difficult job to do.

A big thank you to the Centerville Boys, Todd Flowers, and Jamie Nuzum who gave me my first critiques.

# Table of Contents

## Sharks

I listen to the sound the water makes when she dives beneath its surface. She enters like someone well acquainted with the ocean's movements, intimate with the shifts of tide that ripple over her skin. She swims by the dock, her body the color of a roasted almond in the moonlight. With a long pull of her arm, she beckons me to jump in.

I tell her I'm afraid of sharks. It's night, and swimming in water dark as ink instills a certain fear in me. But she knows this already, the way she knows that I don't like what we're doing, any more than the fact that we're doing it. Maybe that's why I have such an unhealthy fixation with the movie, Jaws. I've seen it at least a dozen times. It fills me with a perverse fascination–the deep ocean shots, the music, the gray torpedo frame speeding through the water. Each time I watch the opening sequence, it's like I'm the one feeling that first bite; being dragged along; the skin tearing loose–blood spurting, my screams jerked down under the water.

All summer, I have come down to this dock and calculated the possibility of a rogue, nomadic shark swimming unnoticed so close to shore, knifing back and forth in the shallow waters.

"There aren't any sharks out here," Emily teases, spitting salt water from her lips. Her arms make wide circles as she treads a few feet in front of me, and her teeth gleam white when she smiles.

I inhale the last of the Pall Malls I stole from Bobby's pack this morning, and reluctantly release the smoke from my mouth. It drifts away in blue twists, disappearing somewhere over the sand. A faint breeze skims off the ocean, blowing hair into my eyes. To my right, Nobska Lighthouse flickers in even intervals, a throbbing reminder.

"No sharks," she repeats.

I remove my shirt and slip off my sneakers, using the toe of one foot as leverage, then the other. My nipples respond when the air touches them and I immediately think of Emily's breasts when I first held them, and of the Pisces tattoo just above her left aureole. For a split-second, I contemplate sliding off my boxer shorts as well, but I know what happens when we're both naked together.

She drifts by completely at ease in her surroundings. There's an inherent grace about her long, fluid movements I know I will never have. She catches me staring, and splashes water onto the dock.

I clench my fingers tightly. Somewhere in the darkness, a buoy bell rings a lonely, judgmental sound.

"Are you coming in or not?" That smile again.

Without another thought, I jump feet first.

*****

My best friend, Bobby, and I unloaded trucks at Kappy's Liquors on Spring Bars Road. Emily worked one of the registers up front. We were all part of the summer help. From time to time, Emily would smile at us while we filled the shelves with large, plastic bottles of vodka and Scotch.

One morning, Bobby nudged me with his elbow. When I didn't respond, he nudged me again.

"Look at that," he said, "She's checking me out."

"Who's checking you out?"

"The girl up there. The blonde."

I glanced over at Emily, who stood by her register, smiling. I turned to the clock on the wall behind us.

"She's checking out the time, you mean."

"She digs me," he said. "I can tell. I know these things."

He laughed and we went back to work. We didn't say another word about it, but the seed had already been planted. I caught her looking a number of times that day, and each time, she'd flash those big white teeth. What's more, I figured out whom that smile was for, and it wasn't Bobby.

It went like that for a week, maybe two. We kept stacking shelves, and she kept smiling at us from behind check-out number two. Once in a while, he hit me on the shoulder and motioned over to her. It was something, I tell you, having a girl look at me like that. Then, a few days later when I was taking inventory before the big road race, I decided to ask her out. Who cared what Bobby thought? Something like this happened once in a lifetime if you were lucky. I marched upstairs and found Emily in the break room sipping a soda through a straw. That's when she told me that Bobby had beaten me to the punch. I froze. It was like someone had kicked me where it counted. I just stood there feeling stupid. Her face saddened, her bright eyes softening in the moment. "Another time," she said. Then she reached out and touched my shoulder the way

women do sometimes to let you know that they care. The fact remained that he asked her out first, and rules were rules, even if they were unwritten; even if there is no magic between two people. So, I played the good friend. What else could I do? I drove when we went to the movies so they could sit together in the back seat. I pretended to be more interested in the action on screen that his hand disappearing between her thighs. Those nights when she stayed over, I feigned sleep or drunkenness while the box spring groaned rhythmically from the other side of the room.

The thing was, every day at work, Emily's eyes followed me wherever I went, whether I was wheeling out a keg, a case of champagne, or if I was just facing down one of the shelves. She'd give me this look–just a glance really, but it told me everything I needed to know.

One night, the three of us got drunk on some Jack Daniels I pinched from the supply room. We drove out to the old Nobska lighthouse on Prospect Road. It was cold, and we took turns passing around the bottle. As it got later, the bottle got lighter. Bobby passed out first. Emily could drink more than any of my friends. I told her this and she laughed. We didn't say anything for a while, listening to the sound of the ocean against the rocks. That's when I told her about my fear of sharks. She listened to me ramble on, maneuvering her face closer and closer to mine so that our lips barely touched.

A couple of days later at work, she found me in the break room having a cigarette. She handed me one of those coffee table books on the Great White. It was filled with the most frightening and wonderful pictures I have ever seen. She watched my face the entire time as I flipped through the pages, eyes blazing, completely consumed by indecency of it all.

There was a short inscription in her handwriting on the inside cover, more of an invitation than a note, and it ended with one word–fuck–then her name.

*****

"I'm not a good swimmer," I say. My hands are heavy in the water, like mallets. They plunk down with every stroke, sending short sprays into my face.

Her body glides by mine underwater. It's long, sleek. My skin tingles when we touch. It's like she belongs here. For a moment, I can't see her, and then her head resurfaces a few feet away. She stands in water waist-high exposing her breasts to the night.

"Come on over here, it's shallow enough to stand."

I take a deep breath and hold it in my lungs as long as possible. Why do I do the things I do around her? I stretch my arms out and claw sloppily through the waves. When I reach her, she leans over and kisses my mouth.

"I love a deserted beach: No one around. The entire ocean to yourself."

She looks around at the beach, then the ocean, then up at the dark sky.

"Look," she adds, "A falling star."

She points and my eyes obey the path of her finger. I catch just enough, an orange ember before it extinguishes.

"Christ, I could use a cigarette right now," I say.

She laughs. It's a sharp sound, like metal on metal.

"What's the difference between a falling and shooting star anyway?" I ask her.

She laughs again, this time, a little louder. She thinks everything I say is funny, including the thing about sharks.

She grabs my hand and places it against the small of her back. Her eyes find mine and refuse to let go. I feel a familiar tug at my groin.

"Hold me," she says.

Before I can ask her what for, she arches backward and surrenders her body to buoyancy. Her breasts loll in the tide and her pubic hair breaks the surface like a strip of blonde seaweed.

"Perception," she says.

I looked at her curiously. "Perception?" I ask.

"A falling star falls because it's used up; a shooting star still has fire inside its belly. Reactive–proactive. It's how you see it: Perception."

With that, she smiles–like it's the simplest definition in the world.

I adjust my hands under her arms and drag her slowly along. She closes her eyes and lets the water run past her shoulders and down over her chest. She is not afraid of drowning. She is someone without fear. She coasts easily, her blonde hair trailing smoothly behind.

"Are you still afraid of sharks?" she asks me suddenly. She keeps her eyes closed. Her face is so relaxed I want to kiss her.

"Always," I reply. "It's good to be frightened of things. Everyone should have at least one fear. Mine is sharks."

"But you're in the water. You're here. You can't be that afraid if you're in here with me."

"More than you know. It's like the Fight or Flight Syndrome. Knowing the possible consequences and escaping them—that gives an incident its meaning."

"That gives an incident meaning, I like that." She thinks this over. "Besides, even if there was a shark in here. There's nothing you can do about it." Then, more seriously, she adds, "Not now."

I continue to pull her around in a circle. In the darkness behind the tree line, the reticence of crickets interrupts the silence in intervals. Their noise fluctuates – loud, soft, then nothing. Loud, soft, then nothing, over and over again.

Suddenly, Emily sits up—then stands in the water.

"What is it? What's the matter?"

"Let's swim to that boat over there," she says.

She points to a motorboat moored about twenty yards on the other side of the small dock. Its silhouette bobs in the distance, its dark bow nodding with the water.

"Race you!"

The space between the boat and us is infinite, or at least a heck of a long swim. If there is a shark here, I wonder if I could make it to the dock before I got eaten, or if I could even make it close.

She splashes water into my face.

"Sissy!"

I rub the sting from my eyes. When I regain focus, she already commands a sizeable head start and is gaining distance. I stand alone, feeling the cold pockets on my legs as I walk blindly in the shallows. I read in the book she gave me that sharks are attracted exactly to the same kind of movements a swimmer makes; that most shark attacks occur in less than six feet of water. They track down their prey, taking them from underneath, and that the pain from even the smallest bite is like lightning searing through your body.

I consider the dark water, the things I can't see. I know better than to follow her, that someone like me can lure a shark with his erratic motion, but I go after her anyway. By the time I reach the edge, she is already on the boat. The recurring thought of being snatched down propels me onto the boat. My teeth chatter and goose bumps pimple my skin.

"You made it," she says, crawling over to me. My heart pumps steadily against my chest. My breath comes in short, panicked, gasps. She wraps her arms around my neck and draws me in.

"My big, strong hero," she whispers before her lips close on mine. I taste the tobacco on her tongue and relish it. She lowers her hand past my stomach and gropes my shorts. I close my eyes and sigh as she bites my lower lip.

*****

Two days ago, in the supply room, it happened. I was carrying a case of schnapps. I didn't hear her come up behind me. I didn't hear anything at all. She must have followed me down the steps. It was like all of a sudden, she was there. She touched my shoulder and I screamed, dropping the case of schnapps on the floor. Bottles of Peachtree exploded when they hit the concrete. Glass and booze went everywhere–my hands, my shoes, all over the floor. The air became thick with that sticky, sweet odor, like blood released into the ocean.

I cut my hands picking up the shards. It looked like I was trying to commit suicide. Red flowed down my wrists and everything became dizzy. And then, she appeared, emerging from the shadows with a roll of paper towels, the Kappy's chevron emblazoned over the left breast of her white work jacket. Without saying a word, she took my hands in hers and kissed my gashes. She licked the blood right off them, her tongue darting in between the separated sections of skin. She let the blood rub against her cheek.

That moment we did it. Right there on the basement floor, amidst the glass and booze and blood. I yanked her skirt up; she popped the button off my jeans. In the pressing urgency of skin on skin, I didn't think of my best friend once; not even when I groaned Emily's name at the end.

*****

Afterward, we stare up at the stars or what remains of them in the night. The salt and sweat cool on our bodies, and our fingertips linger on each other's body in places. I kiss the place where her neck touches her collarbone. It's cold and salty like the ocean.

She rolls to her side, looking at me.

"You know, there is really nothing to be afraid of," she says finally. Her tone is dull, satisfied.

I want to believe her, but I also want to believe none of this ever happened. That's the thing with fear: You either fight it or give into it entirely, there is no middle ground.

"He doesn't have to find out. He won't, not if we don't tell him."

She slides her body over mine and kisses my neck. I rub her back over and over trying to memorize its contours with my touch. I can't convince myself I don't care. He's still my best friend even if I'm not acting like it.

"I've got to tell him," I say. "He has the right to know. I mean, Christ, look at us. It will make everything better."

She pulls away from me and sits with her arms wrapped around her knees.

"It won't solve anything. It won't make a difference, trust me. He'll still hate you. And then what would you have accomplished?"

She looks out at the ocean. She simply stares as if she sees something. Sometimes, she gets like this–unreadable in a way that infuriates me to the point of desperation.

"If the situations were reversed," I press her, "I'd want to know."

"If the situations were reversed, you wouldn't have me."

Her eyes hold a flat, lifeless expression like two small buttons stitched into a doll's face. It lasts only a second, and then just as quickly as it first arrived, it's gone.

"I didn't mean that. God, I hate to argue. Let's not argue anymore, okay? No more fighting. Let's just be who we are. Can we do that?"

She scoots back over to me and wraps an arm around my shoulder. Her skin feels snug and sticky against mine, like things meant to cling together. She touches my lips with her index finger.

"Come on," she pleads softly.

Emilio Iasiello

\*\*\*\*\*

The Carcharodon carcharias, or Great White Shark, eats twice its weight in food every day. It measures up to twenty feet in length, and tips the scales in the vicinity of four thousand pounds. It malignantly courses through the ocean, searching for territory suitable enough to slake its hunger, moving on only when its supply runs scarce. The white shark pins its prey with its lower teeth while at the same time, moving its head laterally to shear off large chunks of its victim with its upper jaws. The entire bite interval happens in a span of less than two seconds, and if you're not lucky, it can mean your life.

She pulls my head to hers and our mouths crush against each other's in the darkness.

\*\*\*\*\*

Somewhere beneath the struggles of the ocean, I can hear a shark feed.

## Why People Do What They Do

John clutches the bottle by its throat and stares out the window of my apartment in Worcester. He carries himself with the quiet satisfaction of a man who knows he's dangerous when he has to be. A slight limp accents his walk where a bullet ricocheted off the floor and shattered his kneecap last spring. Looking at him now, it's hard to believe he'll be only twenty-eight in August. His face consists of hard planes, a solid jaw line, and a nose that has been broken several times above its bridge. He leans close against the glass and stares down at the sidewalk below. Kids' frenzied voices funnel through the torn screen with the Abbot-and-Costello-like banter of "Safe!–Out!" that will signal the end of every stick ball game from now until the end of summer. John keeps peering out the window with a detached look that tells me he's not really paying attention to the events unfolding in front of him. Then, he turns his back on the whole damn sight and walks over to me.

John takes a short swig before he pours some into his glass. He knows how I feel about drinking directly from the bottle and does this more as an afterthought in deference to me than anything else. When he drinks, he kicks the whole bottle back with one tilt of his head. It's scary when he gets like this. Drinking, for him, is like breathing air or fighting. It's not something he does, but something he has to do. He finds a distinct strength in it, something that I neither understand, nor want to, for that matter. Even as a kid, he was either scrapping with someone, or stealing booze from our father's file cabinet. The two images I've carried through much of my life are John passed out or John knocked out, but always on the ground, spread-eagled, blood trickling down his chin. The only difference now, is that he no longer takes ice or water with his liquor. He says he wants nothing to spoil the flavor, although the truth of the matter is that he doesn't want to dull its effects. John is my younger brother, and when he's mad, he drinks hard.

He refills his glass and offers me the bottle.

"Take some," he says. "It's alright for a blend."

I take the Scotch from him and splash a bit into my own glass. It's darker than most, almost like a wild honey color. I raise it to my nose and smell. It has a good, strong aroma that reminds me of our dad.

"What'll we drink to?" I ask him.

He looks at me briefly, and then returns his attention to the window. The children are still out there, only there are fewer of them now. Finally, there's one less kid to scream his head off in this heat.

"Does it matter?" he asks flatly.

I guess it doesn't. When you've been where John has, doing what he has, what you drink to isn't as important as what you're drinking, or how much.

I wince when I see him drinking straight from the bottle again. He glances in my direction, dragging a shirt sleeve across his chapped lips. Then, remembering, adds, "Sorry."

"It's okay," I tell him. He takes another swallow.

* * * * *

John works in a cheap pawnshop down off Flower Street, that is, up until Tuesday, he did. He sat behind a cage and buzzed people in through the front door. The owners kept a loaded shotgun below the counter within reach at all times, "Because in this business, Sweetheart," as John told me one night in his best slurred Bogart voice, "You just don't know."

John has survived two robbery attempts at the pawn shop, one about a year ago, and one just last month. Neither one was successful, but both times the thieves shot him in the process. He has the exit and entrance wounds to prove it–large, fleshy-pink scars that remind you where the living stops and that other thing begins. More importantly, though, John's also been the one to pull the trigger. I've always wanted to ask him what it's like to shoot someone point-blank in the face, but I'm afraid to hear what his answer might be. See, my brother is prone to this type of violence. It follows him like a tail of toilet paper he can't shake off his shoe. He gets banged around from bar to bar only to come up with a fresh set of bruises in the morning. The other thing about my brother is that he always carries out his threats.

Both times, they blamed his drinking. "They" are the family that owns the shop, Iranians or Iraqis, one of those Middle Eastern people whose quick-mart livelihoods depend on the sporadic traffic of consumerism. Zamir is the boss's son and a real son-of-a-bitch. I've met him twice and both times he "yes-sir'd" me to death, smiling in a way I knew he'd rather slit my throat than shake my hand. He said if my brother didn't drink as much as he did, he wouldn't buzz in the "wrong" types of people all the time. By this, I'm sure he means this latest episode as well.

"What the hell is the right type of person to let into a pawnshop?" John asks me.

I shrug. It's a legitimate question to which I have no legitimate answer.

"I've never been inside a pawnshop," I tell him.

"See? That's what I mean. No respectable person goes into pawnshops. Just thieves, sodomites, pedophiles, flashers and drunks."

He takes a big drink after "drunks." The Scotch disappears down his throat in a vacuum of thirst and I watch his Adam's apple bob twice on its way down.

I've never heard John refer to my job at the library as respectable. Mostly, he considers me book-smart in a way he knows he can never be, although he's tried. Once, he even asked me to bring home a few books on the Civil War, but never returned them. I fooled myself into believing that he was taking his time, absorbing dates and battle names, bits of trivia I know he liked. He is my brother. He deserves the benefit of the doubt. A month later, I found them in his apartment trapped under the missing leg portion of his sofa, right next to a bottle of Old Gran Dad. The bottle was, of course, empty.

"It's not like I'm allowed to pat them down or anything. I wouldn't even want to touch half the scum that crawls inside."

"So why did he fire you?" I ask.

"You really want to know, or are you asking the way a big brother is supposed to ask?"

"I really want to know," I say.

He looks at me through gray, anxious eyes to make sure I'm speaking my mind and not just regurgitating something I pulled out of one of the self-help manuals on my shelves, Relieving Stress through Meditation and crap like that. Then, he leans forward and puts one hand on the bottle and lets it rest there. I can tell he feels more comfortable when it's within his reach.

"Okay," he says, "But you got to listen to the whole story."

I tell him I want to listen. He clears his throat.

*****

"This junkie comes in a few days ago, a real low-life. I mean this guy needs a shower like it's nobody's business. I can smell him through the door he smells so bad. Anyway, he comes walking inside, and right off, I can sense something's not kosher about him. I know these things about people. It's my little gift. Some people sense the weather, I sense when someone's not on the up-and-up. Remember what Dad used to say, 'You spend enough time in the gutter, some of it's bound to rub off on you?' Well, this is no different. Like the time I fingered Ritchie Cole for smashing the Galante's window when we were kids. I just know. Anyway, I swear, as God as my witness, if I had seen the tracks up and down this guy's arms ahead of time, I never would have let the bastard in. So in one way, it is my fault."

"What was he looking for?" I ask suddenly.

What people buy in pawnshops has always fascinated me. In Cleveland, when I was ten, we lived over one for six months, and even though there were plenty of times I'd press my face against the glass to look inside, I'd never actually stepped through the front door. The only thing I can figure is that I'm attracted to the indecency of it all. Things which were once sacred are surrendered to the sight and indifference of strangers. It's like going to an antique shop, or garage sale, or wherever someone takes advantage of another person's misfortune. Pawnshops are dirty places where you aren't supposed to go. In this way, I like them.

"He wants to buy a Bowie knife," my brother says finally, pouring more Scotch into his glass. "Like I'm going to sell him that."

I perk up a little in my seat.

"A Bowie knife?" I repeat. "What'd he want with that?"

John lets out a sarcastic laugh.

"I could just imagine looking the way he did and all. Anyway, this junkie must be coming down off his high or something 'cause he starts fidgeting with the buttons on his shirt. He's all fingers, if you know what I mean." He stops for a drink. "Bottom line is, he starts arguing with me because I won't make the sale.

"He has the money and wants to buy the knife. He says he's a big camping fanatic. 'Camping, my ass,' I tell him. 'I'll give you the knife,' I say, 'If you can tell me how to scale a fish'."

I chuckle despite myself. John looks at me sharply. It's important for him to see my eyes when he talks, and I already know this is not a funny story. He picks up the newspaper, looks at it briefly, and then tosses it back on the coffee table. I apologize and let him continue.

"You see what I'm getting at, Bill? I'm sticking to my guns. I got conviction. I'm taking responsibility into my hands like you say I never do. I may be a drunk, but I know what's right and what isn't. Drunks know things even if we never do them."

He pounds his fist against his chest when he emphasizes a point.

"So, no way, I tell him. The knife isn't for sale, at least not for him."

He wets his lips with some Scotch.

"I mean Jesus; I could just picture what this fuck he is going to do with a Bowie knife. You've seen one, so you know what I'm talking about. It's fucking huge. It's got to have a good six-seven-inch blade on that thing. What do you need a Bowie knife in the city for, right? But Zamir hears all the hollering and decides to stick that scrawny neck of his out from his hole in back and get involved. I've told you how Zamir is."

I nod and sip from my glass. Zamir's the type of person you like less and less the more you hear his name mentioned.

"So, the junkie tells him exactly what's happened–I won't make the sale. And the junkie's shaking now, Bill. I mean, he's really shaking. He can't keep it together. His hands are jumping all over the place."

"So what happened?" I manage finally.

He retrieves a cigarette from his shirt pocket. He slaps around his jeans pockets before I toss him my own matches. He lights one and sticks the flame at the end.

"So that son of a bitch tells me–no, he orders me–to sell the guy the knife. How do you like that?"

I don't know quite how to answer, so I drink instead.

"After everything, after the robberies, and his complaints and shit, and all the goddamn crime in this goddamn city, he orders me to sell the knife to a complete freak. And now this guy, Bill, he's got one of those expressions on his face, like 'I'm going to get you when you least expect it' looks and I'm not backing down an inch. No sir, I'm glaring right back in this son of a bitch's face, 'Bring it on, asshole.'"

"I don't think that was a bright move on your part," I tell him.

"Would you can that big brother shit for a minute? This isn't about me, it's about him. Him and that goddamn Zamir."

He throws back what's left in his glass and takes a long drag off his cigarette. He exhales slowly and watches the smoke just barely drift from between his lips. He does this until he's pinching only the filter between his fingers. The smoke lingers like some distorted halo and he looks for images in its curls. He's always liked the motions of smoke, and what the hell, so do I. For a while, neither of us speaks.

that period, I stayed with him every day. John spent three weeks in Saint Vincent's. His wife only lasted one.

She called me a few days later and told me she was taking Maggie away with her.

"What do you mean you're going?" I asked her. "Where?"

"I don't care where," she said. "Just away. I need to be away from this place. I need to be away from him."

Him, she said, like he was some pedophile, not the father of her child.

"Christ, Denise, he needs you more now than ever," I told her, which was the truth. My brother wasn't doing well at all. For a while, the doctors thought he might have a hemorrhage, or worse, permanent brain damage.

"He should have thought about that earlier."

That was it. She hung up. The next time we heard from her was via postcard sent to John from Los Angeles. She neither left a forwarding address nor a phone number, but scribbled "All fine here. Doing well." on it. The picture was an aerial shot of downtown L.A., but the postmark said Nevada.

*****

"You got to put yourself in my position," he says.

John grabs the bottle again and looks as if he's reading the label. Then, he picks up the glass and looks at that, then the bottle, then the glass.

I've known my brother my entire life. And his.

"Someone ought to kill that son of a bitch," he whispers harshly, and for a split-second, I'm not sure if he's referring to Zamir or the junkie.

He tilts his head back and lets the Scotch pour gently out, first in a dribble, then a little more. The hairs on my neck bristle when I hear the dark chug of his throat as he swallows every bit.

As much as I don't want to believe it, I have a sinking feeling that he's right.

Someone will.

## Not My Child

Charlie White Feather and I sit at a table in the corner, away from the others. We split a pitcher of High Life and a pack of smokes. The crowd is small for early afternoon, but should fill up in no time. The plant's second shift gets off work at three. When that happens, it's best to be as far away from the bar as possible. Thirsty factory workers, although good people at heart, have a tendency to be pushy, especially where their booze is concerned. Fights have broken out over the damndest things. If you've ever spent twelve hours punching holes in sheet metal, the last thing you want is something setting you off. Hell, last week, Corky Conlon pulled a knife on Kazursky over quarters on the pool table and they've been best friends since junior high. The sheriff took Corky downtown and locked him up overnight. Next day, Kazursky was there first thing in the morning to bring him to work.

Like I said, we're good people at heart, just don't touch our last nerve.

"Should we get another?" Charlie asks, meaning the beer. He's keeping me from a hot shower and my couch, so he wants to make sure I'm as comfortable as possible. For this, he pays for the rounds.

I glance at the clock nestled between the deer and elk antlers on the wall. It's two-thirty and my daughter won't be home for another half-hour.

"Sure," I say. "But then I got to run."

He flags down Midge and sticks up his finger. "One more."

Midge nods. She never writes anything down. She can remember food orders, soup to nuts, as well as how you like your meat cooked. She also knows how to put a name to a face. She's good that way.

Charlie refills my glass, killing the pitcher as I light another cigarette.

"So what is it you want to tell me?" I ask.

Charlie toys with the smokes. He scratches something in the clear wrapper with his fingernail. Charlie is a big man, with heavy shoulders and steam shovel hands. He's half-Sioux, so his features are dark and menacing. He has long, charcoal-black hair that runs down just past his the collar of his shirt, but the most notable thing about Charlie if you saw him, is the scar from the bottom of his left eye to the middle of his cheek. He doesn't talk about it much, but I know it had something to do with his two year stint in the correctional facility upstate. When you look at him, it's hard to believe that something could make a man of his size so quiet, so much like a child, but I guess everyone has an Achilles heel if you dig deep enough or care long enough to figure it out. Charlie has one. So do I.

Charlie lifts his massive head and stares at me through dark, watery eyes. They shimmer like the black stones in the river we used to fish in near Walpole. I shift uneasily in my chair as my stomach fists itself when I see that look. I know what he's going to say even before he gets a word out.

"My daughter," he says finally, and completely breaks down.

*****

Charlie's daughter, Sunshine, had been going to school with my girl, Sara, since the ninth grade.

They shared the same homeroom for four years, and many of the same classes. For two summers, they both worked part time at Leo's Fashion Warehouse so that during the school year, they could concentrate on becoming "in" or whatever it was that high school girls wanted. At night, it wasn't uncommon for one of them to just show up at the other's house, so it wasn't out of the ordinary to throw an extra plate on the table or remove one depending on which situation presented itself. Sunshine was like having a second daughter, and I know Charlie felt the same away about Sara.

This past year though, something happened. I mean, the two girls drifted apart. Sara ate home more often than not, and I can't tell you how quiet those dinners were. I looked at Sara and Sara looked at her plate. She said she didn't want to talk about it. I told her not to worry, that this wasn't unusual, that things like this happen between friends and interests change.

That's just the way life works out. To tell you the truth, my mind was on too many other things to really give my daughter's problems the proper attention, even if it did concern Sunny, but things down at the factory weren't so good. Rumors were circulating about management cutting back one of the three shifts, which meant lay-offs for a hundred men. I had ten full years in. Even so, whenever money was the motivating factor, no one's position in the pecking order was protected. Too high up meant you could be replaced with two men at the same salary, and if you were too low, well, who needed you anyway?

Since she hit her teens, Sara became the type that gabbed all night on the phone, but when it came to talking to her old man, it was strictly "Yes Dad, no Dad," all the way, so Sara's silence wasn't my top priority. Maybe it should have been, but it wasn't. I'm big enough to admit that.

One day, sometime in late March, I found Sara at the kitchen table in tears. I hadn't seen her crying like that since she found Mary's note on the refrigerator door two years ago. It wasn't much of a note, really, just a torn-out page of the phone book with the words, "I'm so sorry. I love you!" printed in thick, red marker. She had wedged it underneath the watermelon magnet Sara had made for her in the third grade. A fifty-dollar bill was stapled to one corner. I gave her the fifty, but she just tore it up and threw the pieces at me, like it was me who forced her mother into the truck with the Sears guy. Sixteen years is still too young to find things out the hard way, no matter how grown-up you think you are. Sara didn't speak to me for an entire week. She needed to come to grips her own way. I didn't blame her. Who could?

"Honey," I said putting my hand on her shoulder. "What's the matter?"

She lifted her swollen face. Mascara ran down her cheeks in muddy trails.

"It's Sunny," she said sobbing, and then something I couldn't make out.

"What about Sunny? What's wrong? You can tell me."

"This guy she's been hanging out after school with," she said.

That was the big deal? A guy? Here I was, expecting the end of the world and she was crying about boys.

"Honey," I soothed, "don't worry, you'll find someone too."

She just cried louder.

"You don't understand. You don't understand anything! I wish Mom was here!" she wailed, running into her room.

It stung, but there was truth in her words. When it came to important things, nothing I said ever seemed to carry any real weight. It was either too much or too little, but never the right amount. Mary had handled all the minute details–the feminine things, the first kisses and crushes, things of that nature. I was strictly there for the big picture–mortgage, money for new clothes, her college fund. In this way, her mother and I made a great team, but when it came to the day-to-day living, I was out of my element. I walked into Sara's bedroom and found her face down in a pillow.

"Sara," I said, but she just kept shaking her head over and over.

"You don't understand. You just don't understand."

Who knows, maybe I didn't, but what's a father to do? So, I left it alone. I figured things had a way of working themselves out without any interference.

The next day, I had completely forgotten all about it. The plant had posted the cuts and Charlie and I had survived. Sara came home after school, and never mentioned a thing. We sat down to dinner and ate in silence. I even tried telling a few jokes that didn't go anywhere. Then, she talked on the telephone while I cleaned up. It was business as usual.

*****

Charlie told me about the phone calls a few days later over beers at Nellie's. We had just pulled a twelve-hour shift, the upside for not being deemed expendable. I was feeling pretty good despite the long hours. Earlier that day, I had spoken with Jim Murdock in Supply about buying his '89 Shadow for Sara's eighteenth birthday. It was going to be a surprise. I was going to clean up the engine block, adjust the odometer, change the breaks, and replace the tires with four brand, spanking new radials. Then, I was going to leave it for her with a fat red bow in the driveway so she'd find it when she came home from school. We hadn't been getting along too well since the Sunny incident. I mean, she seemed a bit more reserved with me than usual. Maybe I was just making mountains out of mole hills, I don't know, but I wanted to give her something that would really catch her off guard, something she would never expect from her old man.

*****

"What kind of phone calls?" I asked him, lighting a cigarette.

"Strange ones." His voice had a distinct edge to it. He drummed his thick fingers nervously on the tabletop.

"Yeah, but what kind? Hang-ups, heavy breathing, what?"

Charlie clenched and unclenched his fists. His fingers were thick, muscular, scarred from filleting trout on the weekends. He grabbed some peanuts from the wooden bowl. They looked pathetically small in his hands. He held one in between his fingers and squeezed. The peanut made an awful noise, like a neck snapping in two. He ground the remains over the table. Then, he grabbed another and did the same thing.

"I don't know; that's the thing. Someone asks for Sunny and when I ask who it is, they hang-up. Or he does at least."

I laughed.

"Jesus, Charlie, what you got there is a nervous kid afraid of a girl's father," I told him. "Or a prank caller. Hell, we used to prank call girls all the time. It's nothing to lose sleep over."

He shook his head. He pulled on his face with his hands and rubbed a palm over his chin.

"I know a kid's voice, and this wasn't some scared teenager, Stan. This was different. It was a man's voice. I never heard it before, but I'll never forget it. Slippery and cold. The kind of voice you'd half-expect a lizard to have if it talked."

"You're sounding paranoid now," I kidded him. I didn't like where he was going with this. He was really shook up.

Charlie scrutinized the room for a minute, then inspected the grease under his fingernails.

I wanted to ice down the situation a little. "A big half-breed like you paranoid over a stupid voice."

"I am paranoid," he said. "She's my only daughter. You know what it's like to have a daughter."

Then, he showed me something. He opened his flannel shirt to reveal a big bone-handled knife strapped into a leather shoulder harness. It looked old and mystical, with odd bits of turquoise on the hilt, something you might see a chief give his bravest warrior in an old western.

"Jesus, what the hell are you going to do with that?"

"Anything it takes. The Sioux have a saying, Stan." He mumbled something I couldn't understand.

"What's that supposed to mean?"

He didn't respond. He just caressed the bone handle with those large fingers of his, mumbling something over and over in his father's native tongue.

*****

The pictures arrived shortly after, the same day Sunny didn't return home from school. They were in a blank manila envelope wedged between the screen and front doors of Charlie's house. They weren't flattering, I can tell you that. The most decent one of the bunch showed Sunny with this fat hairy guy in a less than favorable position. He could have easily been Charlie's or my age. Neither one was wearing any clothes.

No one could find Sunny. She had gone to school like always, but then disappeared shortly after lunch. No one knew what happened. No one had seen her, could remember seeing her. One minute she was there, the next, she was gone. Just like that, no explanation, no reason.

The teacher told the principal, and the principal phoned Charlie at work.

I was there when he got the call: His face drained of all color and he slammed his fist through the dry-wall. He didn't even bother to hang up the phone before busting out of there. The receiver just dangled on its wire, some man's voice on the other end calling out, "Charlie? Charlie...you there?"

\*\*\*\*\*

Sara was a complete wreck. She didn't go to school for three days. She said she was terrified and I didn't blame her. Once, when I was sixteen, a kid from my school disappeared. No one knew where he went. Kidnapping was eventually ruled out because a ransom note was never sent. Everyone figured him another runaway. The police found him a week later down some ravine near the reservoir. Apparently, he had taken a spill when he was drunk and broke his neck.

I'll never forget the anxiety it caused the town: No one trusted anyone. Parents shuttled their children back and forth to the school. People whispered suspiciously about one another, even in the daylight. It was like fear had put its own personal touch on everyone's shoulder.

Charlie wanted to see Sara. He said she might know something the police missed, anything, no matter how insignificant it might seem. I told him how two detectives had already grilled her for a couple of hours, but he begged me. Those powerful hands of his, hands I had seen crush men's faces with one punch, pleaded for five minutes of her time. Sara said she didn't feel like speaking, but this was important, I told her. After all, this was Sunny's father, my friend.

"There's nothing I can tell you," she said.

"Please, Sara? Anything. Any detail. Who she was seeing. Who asked her out? Anything at all."

"I'm sorry."

"Sara, whatever you know about Sunny you better tell Charlie," I stressed. "For her own sake."

She looked at me with a sense of helplessness.

"She's my best friend!" Then she burst into tears.

Sara told the same story that she'd been telling everyone including the police: Sunny had gradually become more secretive since the beginning of the semester. Instead of hanging out with Sara after school in the afternoon, she'd go off with some man in a black Corvette. She had never met the man and Sunny never talked about him much. She only told Sara that she was doing what she wanted to do. Two days before she turned up missing, Sara saw her getting into his car outside the school gate.

Charlie nodded his massive head as he listened, absorbing each word, each detail, from the man's little moustache to the chipped paint on the passenger-side door. He had Sara repeat things, some two and three times.

I watched him clench and unclench his fingers. I couldn't fathom what it would be like to be in his shoes, to return home one evening and suddenly not know a thing. I tried to imagine how I would feel if Sara had disappeared suddenly one evening, to walk in and not find her books on the floor, or half-eaten celery sticks left out and peanut butter smeared across the counter, but each time, I pushed the thought from my mind. Not my child, I thought. When Charlie finally left, I tucked Sara into bed and gave her two doses of what the doctor had prescribed. I waited for her to sleep and watched her chest rise and fall the entire night, peacefully, like someone without troubles.

The police followed up on the Corvette, but came up empty. They investigated a little further, as much as they could, they said, but ran into one dead end after another. They placed the case in a pending file until further information could be gathered, which, in cop lingo, meant that they had all but officially given up. She was eighteen, they said. She was legally an adult. If she didn't want to be found, she didn't have to be found. They had done all that they could do.

*****

The pictures came each day for another week or so. There was nothing on the envelope, no postmark, no stamp, no anything, just a plain, brown envelope with dirty pictures inside. The last one had a videocassette. Fifty minutes of the most painful stuff a father could watch his daughter do. I know. Charlie showed it to me. I sat in his recliner, the pastrami I had eaten for lunch rising to my throat. I didn't know what to say. It was God-awful. When I tried to shut it off, he grabbed my arm, swallowing my entire wrist in his palm. I couldn't help but think that if he had squeezed hard enough, he could have snapped it, just like the peanuts.

"Just watch," he said grimly, his face focused on the glow of the screen.

I watched Sunny in a frightening variety of sexual misconduct. She did stuff that you couldn't find in most video stores; I'm talking about things I had only heard about or read about or seen advertised in the back of low-grade skin magazines. My stomach made uneasy noises. I felt sick. I had held this kid in my arms when she was born. Now, she was doing things I couldn't imagine one human being doing to another.

Charlie just kept his dark eyes fixed to the screen. I don't think he saw what she was doing as much as he was searching for something in his little girl's face. Some mark of pain, bruises, scars, some anger or frustration burning beneath her eyes. That was the thing. Maybe, if she had shown some resilience, some displeasure, it could have been resolved, but there wasn't any. There was nothing that hinted that she wasn't having anything but a good time.

I barely made it to the bathroom before I lost it. When I came out, Charlie was there with his thumb on the remote, stopping the tape and rewinding.

Stopping and rewinding.

\*\*\*\*\*

The police still did nothing about it.

"No crime's been committed. There's been no intent, no threat of violence. The most you have here are some dirty pictures of your adult-aged daughter," a young detective told him. There was nothing that they could do, they assured him. Their hands were tied.

A few days later, everything stopped. No more pictures, no more videotapes. It was like nothing had ever happened. Just poof, and everything was gone. There was still no sign of Sunny. She never wrote or called. None of the hospitals or morgues turned up anyone fitting her description, so as far as we knew, she was alive somewhere. Sunny was alive and making pornographic material.

\*\*\*\*\*

Things finally went back to normal, or at least as normal they could get. Sara returned to school. She never talked about the incident after that night and I never pressed her. I was just glad that she seemed to have moved past everything. She joined a few school functions in the afternoons to keep from being idle, at least that's what she told me. I believed it was because she didn't want to think about her friend, which was okay with me. The situation was unnerving to say the least.

Sara's eighteenth birthday came and went. She still didn't say much around the house. She stayed in her room mostly, or else she watched a little TV with me at night. The few times I'd walk into the kitchen and find her on the phone, she'd turn her back to me, whisper something and then hang up quickly. When I asked her about it, she would just say it was a friend and leave it at that. I told myself she was acting this way because of Sunny. I mean, it's not like Sara was a recluse. She went on occasional dates, but nothing serious ever came out of them. Some of the boys were pretty nice too, but all she would ever say about them was, "he's a jerk," or "not my type."

It was about this time when rumors started floating around work about a Japanese company interested in buying the plant and all hell broke loose. For two weeks, union reps called meetings during the evenings at the local Knights of Columbus. I'd see Charlie sitting on one of the benches, not so much listening as just staring ahead.

Sometimes he'd sit next to me.

"You got to let this go, Charlie," I told him one night.

He said he knew I was right. He was trying, but it was tough.

I said I know.

We left it at that.

I started to see less and less of my daughter. She skipped dinners to go to study groups the few nights I did make it home. I was a little hurt by that, but it wasn't like I was exactly around a whole lot either. I was busy picketing, or collecting signatures down at the Safeway. But hell, she was already into the state college, so why shouldn't she have her fun? So I let it go.

A month or so passed. The Japanese company bypassed us in favor of a more "receptive" company in the next state. Charlie and I worked our shifts like always, talking about sports, the latest trades, the play-offs, what have you. He thankfully never brought up Sunny again which made me happy as I never knew what to say about it, especially with graduation coming up in a month. As far as I could tell, he was moving past it, as much as he would allow himself. Sometimes, I'd catch him staring off into space, and I knew he was recalling Sunny's face, not the one in the pictures or the movie, but the way she used to look, all smiles, the one joy in his life.

*****

This afternoon however, he came up to me, his face flushed, urgent.

"I got to talk to you," he said.

"What about?" I asked.

He looked around at the other men, and then leaned in close. I caught some of their looks. Some of them whispered and others just shook their heads.

"After work," he said.

And I got that feeling all over again.

\*\*\*\*\*

Midge brings over the fresh pitcher. There's a slight head to it and the glass beads up with moisture, then drips down the sides.

I grind out my cigarette and immediately light another. I don't like the look in his eye. He's thinking too much, not knowing what words to put together.

"Just say it," I tell him.

He produces a manila envelope from the seat beside him.

"I got some more," he says. "They were waiting for me at the gate. Someone dropped them off. The guard couldn't remember what he looked like, but he remembered the car sure enough: a black 'Vette."

He places the package in front of me. I want to look at it, but at the same time, I don't. Charlie has had some rough moments; times when I thought he'd just go ballistic.

I've seen him smash his fist against the wall over and over again, his knuckles splitting open, wood splinters spearing into that raw, bloody flesh, then fall to the ground crying like some helpless child, but each time he has pulled through. The last thing he needs now is more pictures to remind him of everything. I know I don't want to be reminded. I don't want to see a kid I've known since she was a baby engaged in this type of life. You see an infant and all that you can think of is what they could be. You never think of how they will turn out.

I glance at the clock on the wall and clear my throat.

"I'd like to stay, Charlie, really, but I got to get back," I tell him. "Sara's going to be home soon." It's pretty much the truth. Usually, she gets home, does her homework, and I watch TV while she talks on the phone. Tonight is going to be different. She's supposed to cook my favorite dinner–pork chops and gravy–as a thank you for putting up with her mood swings the past couple of months. I told her she didn't have to, but she insisted. She also told me to rent a movie for later and we'd make popcorn. It would be just the two of us spending a nice, quiet evening at home. I was looking forward to this. I haven't looked forward to something in a long time.

"Stan," he says before I stand fully up. "Where is Sara now?"

"School stuff," I reply and then choke on a sip of beer. "Yearbook or something like that."

He puts one hand over mine. The palm is hot, sweaty. At quick glance, it looks as if I have a stump instead of a fully functioning limb.

"I think you better take a look at these," and hands me the folder.

I sort through the photos. They're like stills from a perverted movie. First, there's Sunny alone, then Sunny and a man, then Sunny and two men. The action escalates to such a degree that if you ran a thumb over the corners of all fifteen, they would suddenly spring into life. There's even an animal that looks like a dog in one.

"So?" I say, swallowing hard.

Then, I see it before he gets it out of his mouth. There, next to Sunny in the last picture, I see her lying on the bed next to an open window, legs spread, her mouth frozen in what looks to be a laugh–high and frivolous–a sound I haven't heard from her in a long time.

"Stan," he says again, but I'm far away from him now, pulled into that picture with my daughter and her friend, and two men I've never seen before. My daughter is naked, rolling around, doing things. And laughing. That's the worst part. That's what gets me the most. My daughter is laughing, hard and loud, like nothing in the world could stop her.

## Say Something

We're fighting again. Arguing about something, I don't know what. I did when we first started yelling, but things have a way of piling up. One thing leads to another, which leads to another. You understand how it goes. What starts over dishes in the sink can turn into a completely different monster altogether. By this, I mean this latest episode as well.

We're both in the kitchen smoking cigarettes. I had quit for a couple of months, but I started again recently. Smoking is not good for you, but neither is sex, at least, not now it isn't. It seems that anything can kill you if it wants to. Or if you let it. At least I had changed brands. It's a step in the right direction, a way of moving past something that no longer has meaning.

We used to smoke the same kind, me and her. It didn't matter which pack you took from. Now, there're two different types of butts in the ashtray.

"Something has to give," Janie says.

I crack the window to let the smoke have a way out instead of hanging in the space between us. I watch it filter into the open air, curling briefly before dissipating into the night. For a second, I feel a jealous twinge. I'd give anything to be able to slip away just like that, to be out of this situation, any situation. Janie has just finished saying something else. Her eyes are red, the whites all bloodshot. She has cried once already and I'm not sure what she's about to do now. She's waiting for me to say my piece. Thing is, I don't have any piece to say. I have nothing to tell her, nothing that she wants to hear. She keeps looking at me expectantly. That's when the phone rings.

"Hello," I say, picking up the receiver.

"Baby? That you?"

The voice is a slow, Southern drawl, rough on the edges. She's drunk again. She calls me when she gets like this.

"Lee," I sigh.

Janie throws up her arms in disgust.

"Again? For heaven's sake, she called last night," she says. "When is she going to leave us the hell alone?"

Janie doesn't understand. She thinks I'm having something on the side with this woman. Fact is, I've never touched her, at least, not physically. Lee is in my writing class at school. She's an older woman, mid-fifties, a smoker just like us. She's also run the gambit–married, divorced and widowed. You name it, she's been there. Thing about Lee–the thing that I noticed right off–is that she dresses elegantly for someone taking night classes. She wears jewelry and gets her hair done just so, while the rest of the women wear sweat pants and baggy pull-overs. Lee doesn't work either. Husband number two has taken care of that. If she doesn't want to see another job, she doesn't have to, that's how well-off she is. But money isn't everything, and that's the truth. Money doesn't take care of the boredom when you're alone. It doesn't take care of the hours in-between, so Lee decided to go back to school. Honestly, I admire her for doing what she's doing. It takes courage to walk around campus where everyone else is less than half your age and wondering if you're some parent looking for your son or daughter. Hell, I'm a good six years older than most of the others in my class and Lee has me beat by at least fifteen. She's even older than our professor.

I liked Lee from the start. She's no-nonsense. She's seen and experienced things most of us haven't even imagined yet, things that seem only to happen to people on TV. She gives a different perspective to the class, something beyond the confines of Generation X. She isn't afraid to say what she thinks and why. Sometimes, she brings in old newspaper articles and magazines to pass around–first published stories by Salinger and Hemingway, poems by Sexton and Plath. Before she was married (the first time), she wrote a couple of book reviews for *The New Yorker* back when *The New* Yorker was the only game in town. Lee's experience gives her an authority our teacher doesn't have, will never have, but there are times it doesn't.

My girlfriend raises her hands. Her face is pained, frustrated. What can I tell her?

"Talk to me, Lee. What's the matter?"

"There you go again." Lee says, "Lee, Lee. That's all you ever say. Don't you understand where I'm coming from?"

I tell her I don't. There is a long pause, and for a minute, I think she might hang up.

"Are you still there?" she says, attitude edged in her tone.

"Of course I'm here," I say. "You called me, remember?"

"I don't need your charity, if that's what you think! I'm not a damned invalid, you know." The booze makes her voice sound different, more throaty, like Lauren Bacall. Her voice sounds husky in a sexy way, not a manly one. She pauses. Through the phone, I hear her strike her lighter.

"Of course you're not. I don't know why I said it."

My girlfriend bangs around some pots and pans in the kitchen. She's like a child demanding attention. She doesn't understand other people's problems. She refuses to look beyond her own narrow scope. I told her that once before and she nearly flipped out. She almost stabbed me with a serving fork. I've never seen her so angry. It was like something fragile inside her had suddenly snapped.

I put a finger in one ear and move to the other side of the kitchen.

"Good God, what's all that racket?"

"Janie," I tell her. "She's pissed at me."

"What the hell is she pissed at you for?" Lee asks. "She's the one making all the Goddamned noise."

"It's a long story. I really can't stay on the phone long."

"Oh sure, I understand. I understand completely. I was married too once. Hell, more than once, thrice." She laughs.

"I'm not married," I say a little too loudly, then look over at Janie. She has taken out a honeydew from the fridge and is now eyeing the cutlery. She grabs one of the handles and slides the blade out part-way. Then, she replaces it and pulls out another.

"Look, I don't mean to be short, but–"

"So did you give any thought to what I said?"

"About what?"

"You know," she says.

Janie raises the large knife above her head with both hands then splits the melon in half. It makes an awful, hollow sound. It's almost like a scene from a movie–the Arabian executioner bringing down the scimitar, the next victim watching the horrible sight.

Janie shoots me an angry look when she knows I'm looking. Still glaring, she scoops out the seeds with a spoon.

"Lee," I say.

"Come on, Baaaabbby."

Janie raises the knife again and quarters the halves.

*****

I can't recall exactly when things with Janie had taken a turn for the worse, but if I had to pinpoint a moment, it would be the start of the semester. I had told her that I wanted–needed–to go full-time. There were no two ways about it. I had to give my complete attention to school. I just didn't "fit" in with the rest of my class. I felt no link to the other students. She wanted to know why the hell I needed to feel a link in the first place. She didn't get it. I explained to her that this was important. Writers needed to be close to each other, that's what I said. They needed the backing of someone who knew the score, who had tackled the same situations. I told her I had missed too many opportunities already: Too many readings by famous authors, too many get-togethers after class. I told her my job had eaten up too many of my hours and my writing suffered as a consequence. A decision had to be made, I said, and this was it. My mind was fixed.

She didn't say much at first. She calmly lit a cigarette with my lighter, squinting her eyes as she did when she was thinking. Then, the storm hit. Why couldn't I work part-time? Why did I have to burn every bridge I crossed? Why did I always have to throw away a sure thing? We went back and forth like this all night. Finally, push met shove. I told her if she really loved me–really believed in what I was doing– that this was the only way. She said I wasn't being realistic. She said some other things as well, but in the end, she relented. She agreed to put me through my remaining semesters. She paid for my tuition out of her checking account, and when I had to buy books for class, I used her credit card, signing my name on the dotted line.

\*\*\*\*\*

Lee started calling me about a month and a half ago. At first, it was simple things–a homework assignment, a phone number, a copy of the class list. Then, we started talking about other things: Who our favorite authors were, our primary influences, if any. Was Hemingway really gay? We talked for hours about harmless stuff. It felt good to be regarded as a peer by someone of her obvious experience. There was a certain prestige in it, like being privy to something the others weren't. On breaks, we'd stand outside, apart from the rest of the class, like old soldiers who had covered the same piece of ground, but in different wars. Sometimes, when she'd call, we'd lose track of time altogether.

"Lee," I'd tell her on the phone, "it's almost one. I got to get some sleep."

She'd apologize and start to hang up, but then catch another tangent and before we knew it, another hour would fly by. In the beginning, Janie used to kid me about it.

"She has a crush on you," she said out of the blue one Sunday morning.

I put down the paper and looked at Janie. It was something I hadn't considered before. It was such a strange thought–a woman almost twice my age having a thing for me. I had to admit, it was a flattering concept. For a while there, I couldn't get images of Anne Bancroft in *The Graduate* out of my head.

I turned to Janie, who was fixing herself another cup of coffee.

"She's just lonely," I said finally. "Her third husband died a few months ago. Besides, it's not like it's really possible. I mean, Christ, she's like fifty-something."

"I know women," she said. "And it doesn't matter how old she is. She could be Methuselah and she could still have the hots for you."

Maybe she did, and maybe she didn't. At the time, I didn't know. I told Janie she was crazy, but the whole conversation got me thinking. Lee was attractive; there were no two ways about it. She always wore these sharp, classy outfits—silk blouses and short skirts. She rarely wore pants. When the next Thursday night rolled around, I watched her from across the room, crossing and re-crossing those fine legs. I remembered her mentioning something about playing tennis three times a week and her legs showed it. They were firm without being overtly muscular. Her calves still kept their shape. Hell, I'd be lying if I said I didn't give what Janie said any thought. Fact is, I had already pictured having sex with Lee long before Janie said anything. There was just something about her. She had the type of skin I knew my hands had never felt. In my defense, I had never actually considered acting on those ideas. They were just harmless thoughts, little daydreams to get me through the long lectures on Chekhov and Gogol.

\*\*\*\*\*

The first major incident between me and Janie involved the movies. There were others, I'm sure, but this one sticks out. It was Wednesday and I was working on something that I had to pass out for class the next night. It was hard going, but there were places where the writing went smoothly. It was the kind of writing that you had to fight for word by word, but if you put the time in, the product was its own reward. So I kept on this way–typing, reading, typing, reading– until Janie walked through the door waving around something in her hand.

"Do I have a surprise for you," she said.

She walked over to the table and tossed her purse down on a few of my papers. She helped herself to a cigarette and lit it.

"Well, aren't you going to ask me what it is?"

By that point, it was too late. I had lost my train of thought. I removed my glasses and rubbed my eyes.

"What is it?" I asked her.

She showed me two white pieces of paper.

"Tickets, for the seven o'clock show." She glanced at her watch. "You have a few minutes to wash up and change that shirt. Aren't you excited? I can't remember the last time we went to the movies."

I put my glasses next to the typewriter.

"Honey, I can't. I'm writing here."

"You've been writing every night. Can't you just take a break for two hours?"

"You don't understand. I'm writing. There's a rhythm involved. If I stop now, I might not get it back."

"What about our rhythm, Harold? When are we going to get back into our rhythm?"

"Janie," I said.

"Don't 'Janie' me, I'm serious. I've done my part. I've given you space. I've put up with all your late-night shenanigans on the phone with your classmates to all hours. I don't think I'm asking the world here. A fucking movie, Harold, two measly hours. To feel like we're still together. Did it ever occur to you that I need to believe that I'm a part of something?"

"You are, Sweetheart. You are."

She shook her head.

"No. It's just you and this thing you're doing."

"Honey."

"Forget I even asked. Do what you want, Harold."

With that, she walked out of the room, slamming the door behind her. Ten minutes later, the phone rang. It was Lee.

"What you doin', Baby?" she said.

*****

Things started going downhill fast from then on. Don't get me wrong, we were headed down this path long before Lee entered the picture. Still, little things began to get on each other's nerves. For instance, the Saturday after the movie fiasco, when I was in the library, Janie rearranged the cupboards in the kitchen. She didn't just clean them out, no; she moved things, completely switching shelves, condensing space. It was a Herculean effort. She emptied everything and started fresh. When I got back, I couldn't find a goddamn thing. Things were in total disarray–soup cans where the spaghetti sauce used to be, tortilla chips instead of Captain Crunch. Nothing was where it once was. Finally, when I slammed a cupboard door–we erupted. She started shouting, and then I started shouting.

We both said some things we didn't mean, or maybe we did mean them, I can't be sure. Then, the stuff about Lee resurfaced and the whole scene turned ugly.

When I told her she didn't understand other people's problems, that was the last straw. She grabbed the closest thing at hand–a serving fork–and came at me with it like a street fighter with little time on her hands. She jabbed the fork at me in short, quick bursts.

If she hadn't stumbled over the mat by the sink, I'm sure she would have run me through.

But it wasn't her fault: I knew she wasn't thinking straight. She wasn't a person normally given to this type of violence. After we both cooled down, I tried to explain to her that I was a person that needed things the way they were. I needed room. I liked to be able to poke around my cans without having them pressed together in tight rows. She said it made more sense to condense, to save space for more things, to economize.

It was too late and we both felt it. We had passed something, me and her. You don't try to kill someone one moment, and then make plans for the future the next. Janie grabbed my pack, walked out onto the balcony, and smoked a cigarette. I watched her through the sliding glass door, bringing the cigarette to her lips in staccato bursts that made me think of the fork again. It was another argument in which we didn't say what was really on our minds.

*****

About a week later, Lee started calling me while she was drunk. I felt sorry for her. I figured she was lonely and she just needed to talk it out. So, she did. She went on about her life as if reciting a resume; the jobs she had, the bosses that tried to sleep with her, her time at New York City's posh Cosmopolitan Club, snipped of her life, nothing really important.

Then, five days ago, our conversations took a different turn.

Monday, she called me around eight o'clock.

Janie was out some place; where, I don't remember or don't know. She had stopped offering me the particulars of her life. I had been sitting around, staring at the typewriter or drinking, probably both.

"Baby, that you?" That voice again: Thick and slurred like maple syrup. It sent shivers in my belly.

"Baby, you there all by your lonesome?"

I told her I was.

Then, Lee started saying things. She told me what she was wearing: A red satin robe, open, nothing else. That's what she said, word for word. She said other things as well, hot and desperate things. I got excited and said some things back to her.

It went like that on Tuesday too, and Wednesday. It got so it became a game between us. I could picture her sitting in her leather recliner, legs spread wide, with a glass of Tom Collins in her hand and I'd tell her what I'd do if I was there. Then, we actually took turns saying what we'd do, going back and forth, and then doing it on ourselves. It got so I was taking off my clothes and imagining Lee's fingers on the buttons.

"I'm smoking too," she said in a deep growl. "You know how my mouth gets when I smoke."

*****

But then things turned weird. I mean, they started getting personal. Before I knew it, the fun stuff stopped and she was telling me things about her life I didn't need to know, didn't want to know.

"I was raped by my father when I was thirteen," she blurted out twenty minutes into the conversation on Thursday. "Once a week, he'd bring me to my piano lessons. Then afterward, we'd go get ice cream. That was his code for it, you know. Getting ice cream. One push and my innocence just disappeared. I couldn't eat ice cream for twenty fucking years after that."

I didn't know what to say. What could you tell a person after that?

"Jesus, Lee."

"It gets better. Later, he divorced my mother and ran off with another man. Another man, for Christ's sakes. After doing what he did to me for God knows how long. Go figure that."

I said nothing. I paced around the kitchen. I looked out at the street. Every once in a while, a car passed by. I didn't want to talk about this. I didn't know what to say. I fumbled for a cigarette.

"Why are you telling me this?"

She didn't answer. She just kept on with her stories, each one more bizarre and disturbing than the previous one.

She had a brother who turned out to be a transvestite. He was later killed by a male lover in a jealous rage. The police found him in a run-down motel room in Atlantic City dressed in a lace bodice and stockings. He was strangled by a pair of his lover's crotchless panties. Lee had to drive four hours there to claim the body. She described every detail, the blue eye-shadow on her dead brother's face, the smeared lipstick, the torn lobe where an earring was ripped out.

If that wasn't bad enough, her first husband, Jimmy, was an alcoholic with a taste for kiddy porn.

"He never actually touched them, heaven forbid," she made sure to tell me, "He only liked to watch. He had a special room and everything. After dinner, he'd retire there, sit in a high wing-backed leather chair and watch tape after tape. One of his kinks was to dress me up like a school girl–complete with pig tails, uniform, and knee socks. He called me funny names–Susan, Betty, Ashlee. It was all very strange. Very strange."

By all counts, I should have been repulsed, but I felt sorry for her. And the more sorry I felt, the more I listened. And the more I listened, the more excited I became.

She kept talking. My hands were shaking. I undid my pants like before.

I listened. I listened hard.

\*\*\*\*\*

"You can do it, Baby," she said to me last night.

"Do what, Lee?"

"Write my story. It's quite a story. Rape, incest, homosexuality, you name it, it's got it. I got more skeletons than a graveyard."

Janie was standing in the corner of the living room, her arms folded across her breasts. She was smoking and looking out the window. The subject of sex came up again. She had concerns that the flame of our relationship had extinguished, and she was right.

We hadn't been together since school had started up. I told her it was the stress, but we both knew I was lying.

Two nights ago, she came home drunk. She had been out with the people from her office. It was late, almost two. I was lying in bed. I had just gotten off the phone with Lee when I heard the car pull into the driveway. I smelled it on her breath the moment she climbed on top of me. Her eyes were glassed over, not really focused. She leaned over and forced her tongue into my mouth. The mixture of cigarettes and booze made my stomach turn one cartwheel after another. She grabbed my crotch.

"You want some lovin', Baby?"

I quickly looked at her. Baby! Fear rippled through me. Did she know? Had she overheard one of my phone escapades? Had she seen something?

Baby.

"What did you say?" I asked her, gripping her wrist tightly.

She made a face. "That hurts," she said. Suddenly, I knew she didn't know a thing. She was just talking. She was just drunk. I lay back down on the bed, sighing heavily. I felt foolish, guilty. The terror subsided.

"Come on, you up for a little ass or not?" She ground her hips into me.

I didn't know what to say. There was a time, I'm sure, when I thought that Janie was the most beautiful woman in the world. There was something about her that must have attracted me once–something beyond her obvious physical beauty, something that if asked, I couldn't put my finger on. I tried to explain it to her long ago, but couldn't quite describe it. It was something impalpable; forged inside her the moment she was born, as if an angel had touched her while she was inside the womb. Lying there with her on top of me, I looked for it again. I kept looking.

"What have we here?"

She rubbed my crotch too hard, racking my balls. I groaned. She mistook it for pleasure and did it harder. I grabbed her hand and twisted it back.

"Fucker!" she hissed, scratching my shoulder with her nails. She did it hard and deliberately, and she drew blood. I swore and let go. She climbed off of me and stood in front of the bathroom door. "You son-of-a-bitch, fucker! What the fuck's the matter with you?"

I dabbed my shoulder with a corner of the sheet and looked at it. Large blots of crimson spread over the whiteness. I carefully touched the flaps of skin and wondered if I needed stitches or not.

"That woman is destroying our lives!"

"Janie," I said.

"I want to know what the deal is, Harold! What's happened to us? What's happened?"

I didn't know what to say. It was a good question. There was something missing, that was for sure. Janie had had it. She looked at me through wild eyes. Her hair was mussed up. Her face issued a challenge.

"It's her or me. You need to decide."

I dabbed my shoulder. It stung with each touch.

"Well?" she said. "Are you going to answer me?"

\*\*\*\*\*

"Now's really not the best time, Lee," I tell her.

Janie has stopped cutting. There's a look on her face as if she's calculating something. She leans on the island with both hands, one of which still holds the knife. At a quick glance, she looks like a knight after a battle or a gladiator about to step into the arena.

"Is there ever? Trust me when I tell you this– there ain't ever a best time. But you can write this for me, Baby. You can bring my tragedy to life."

"What for? Why would you want this public?"

"There's a reason you don't see ghosts in the daylight."

"Are you seeing ghosts?" I ask her.

"Baby, aren't you?"

"Harold, we have things to talk about," Janie says. She has cut up the honeydew and added a few peaches and bananas as well. She has tossed them all into a bowl and covered it with saran wrap. Janie has nervous energy. She's one of those people who can't stop doing things. She can never just relax.

I cover the mouthpiece with my hand.

"What do you want me to do?"

"I want you to hang up the damn phone!"

"You don't understand," I tell her.

"There's nothing to understand," she says, her voice rising. "We need to talk, to discuss things. And you–"

"Me what?"

"Are you there?" Lee says. There's a hint of annoyance in her voice.

I tell Lee to hang on. Janie screams. It's loud, high-pitched, the whine of an animal caught in a trap when it realizes that it will have to chew its own leg off to escape. She still has the knife in her hand. For a split-second, I think she may attack me with it, just like the fork. Given the past, there's always that chance.

She beats both fists on the island in the kitchen.

"Talk to me, Harold! To me!"

"Baby? Say something! What's going on? Are you listening? Are you there or not? Talk to me!"

Two women are screaming. Their voices are loud and run over one another. It's difficult to determine where one ends and the other begins. I look at Janie, then the phone: Janie, the phone.

"Talk to me, damn it!" one of them shouts, "I'm right here!"

## Just Us

Joe is a little drunk. He opens another bottle of red wine for us, something French. He flashes me a bit of a smile as he works out the cork. He grips the neck with his left hand, and wiggles the corkscrew with his right. His wife, Cheryl, and my girlfriend, Maggie, sit across from each other as he and I do. Cheryl, like Joe and me, is finished eating. Only Maggie still pecks at the little remains that are left. She has already picked through my plate and has now moved on to the serving dish.

"Anyone want this?" she asks, spooning out the last brown lump of Chicken Marsala.

"I couldn't eat another thing," I say, pushing my plate aside for emphasis.

"All yours, Baby-doll," Cheryl says.

Joe pops the cork and goes around the table with the wine. This third bottle is his idea. I like Joe because he's not afraid to please. Too often, I've noticed that people our age have stopped drinking altogether, as if it makes you an outcast that you like to hit the bottle once in a while. In college, these people drank like fish; now, it's all temperance and snide remarks. Take last week for instance: I went up to Boston to visit an old college friend who hadn't touched alcohol in over a year. When we went out to a bar, he drank coke all night, while I ordered scotch and soda. He said it didn't bother him, but it sure as hell bothered me. When you're drinking, nothing's worse than being with someone who isn't, or someone who's afraid to. I don't know if that makes me an alcoholic or just a pain in the ass. People have showed me evidence for both.

But not Joe. He likes his drink as much as he likes his food. We've often joked that the reason we all get along so well is because of our indulgences. Hell, I figure it could be a lot worse. We could be into heroin or pedophilia, not that anyone I know is, but you hear things.

Cheryl gets up to clear the dishes, but Joe puts a hand on her arm.

"Where's the fire?" he asks, and everyone laughs.

Cheryl looks at Maggie and me and smiles.

"Joe doesn't like to rush things," she says, sitting back down.

"That's right," he says. "I like to take my time. The rest of the week is for rushing around. Good food, good wine. That's what it's all about."

He looks at me a moment, and scratches the back of his head. "You're the writer. What's that saying about living, Mike? You know the one I'm talking about. If you live well, it's the best thing. Something like that."

"Living well is the best revenge?" I offer.

"That's it. Living well is the best revenge. No truer words have been spoken."

For a few seconds, no one says anything. Joe and Cheryl are Maggie's friends, sweethearts since high school. Maggie likes them because they make her believe in the possibilities of love. Maggie was engaged once to her high school sweetheart, but things didn't pan out the way it did with these two. When we first started dating, she was open about the whole thing. She told me that when push came to shove, she and Darren wanted different things. I told her most people wanted different things, but she said it wasn't the same. She went on about irreconcilable differences or some nonsense like that. Then she said she had terminated her pregnancy. She said it was the hardest thing she ever had to do. Darren wasn't too far behind that. I couldn't argue with her. Nothing like that had ever happened to me, so what could I tell her?

"I read an interesting story in the paper today, did either of you catch it?" Joe says. He sits back in his chair and folds both hands behind his head.

I shake my head.

"Missed it," Maggie says, lifting the fork to her mouth.

"It's about this guy up in German-town. Thursday night, he and his wife were walking home from a restaurant. It was nice night like tonight. They had just finished a good meal, Chicken Marsala, or whatever. They were minding their own business, holding hands, when all of a sudden, this kid comes out of nowhere with a gun and sticks them up."

"Awful," Maggie says, chewing with her mouth open. She looks at Joe, then me, to see if we share her reaction.

Joe adjusts himself on the chair.

"Wait, I'm not finished yet. It gets better–or worse, depending on your viewpoint. So," he says, "this kid comes out of the alley or wherever, gun in hand and tells the couple he's going to shoot them if they don't walk into the alley with him. You know, to get out of the street where people can see them."

He pauses and reaches for the Merits and the matches.

"Anyway," he says flipping out a filter, "there the couple is, scared shitless I'm sure, with this kid waving around a gun. So the guy, the husband, he hands the kid his wallet. 'Take it,' he says, 'just don't hurt us.' But the kid isn't listening. The kid, I mean, he's just standing there, checking out the poor guy's wife, if you know what I mean. And right away, this poor bastard knows what's going through the kid's mind."

"Oh, God, I don't know if I want to hear this story," Cheryl says, digging out a cigarette for herself. "You know I don't like these stories."

"Me neither," Maggie says. "I don't like to hear awful things."

Joe blows a trail of smoke out the corner of his mouth.

"But it can happen. Am I right?"

"That doesn't mean it's not awful," Maggie says, putting her fork down.

"Now look what you made her do," Cheryl says.

"No, I'm all right, really. I was finished anyway."

"Oh geez. I'm sorry. I didn't mean to," Joe says. "Really, go ahead and eat. I'll wait 'til you're done."

"No really, I'm stuffed."

Maggie grabs the cigarettes and lights one for me, then one for herself. She's considerate this way.

She always makes sure I have my food, my drink, whatever. The last girl I dated didn't even know I was in the room half the time, but not Maggie. She's got that instinct.

"But wait, just hear me out. This all has a point. Trust me, okay? So this kid tells the guy to get down on the ground face-first. And the man is hesitating. He doesn't want to, but he doesn't exactly have a whole hell of a lot of choice. So he just stands there looking at his wife who is looking back at him. And you know a lifetime passes between them in that look."

"Jesus," I say, shaking my head.

"Now remember, this kid has a gun. He's dangerous. Hell, for all this guy knows, he's trigger happy, or crazy on drugs or something." Joe pauses to exhale. He doesn't take the cigarette out of his mouth.

He squints a bit as the smoke climbs up into his face.

"What do you think he does, or better yet, what would you do?"

"Oh, Honey," Cheryl scolds him rubbing his shoulder. "He always does this. These little games. Don't you, Honey?"

"This isn't a game," Joe says. "I mean it is, and it isn't. But this really happened. I'm curious to know what Mike would do. Hell, what would anyone do?"

Joe sits back in his chair and studies our faces. He grabs the bottle and pours himself some more wine, then looks to see if anyone's glass needs more.

"Tick-tock, tick-tock," he says.

"What else could you do?" Maggie says. "You do what he says. He's in control of the situation. Whoever has the gun makes the rules."

"Well, there's one thing I forgot to mention. And Mike, I think you can appreciate where this is going. The kid, see, makes the guy an offer. He says, 'I can kill you now or I can let you live, but either way, I'm going to get at your wife.'" Joe puts both of his elbows on the table. "So the fact remains–what would you do?"

"Joseph's had too much wine," Cheryl says. "Don't pay attention to him."

She gives Joe a playful pat on the head.

"Yes, I've had a lot of wine, but the question still stands. It's kind of like something out of Hitchcock, you know? I mean, I know what I'd do, because I'm me. But what would someone else do? What would you do? See what I'm getting at? It's a tough situation, but a realistic one because it happened. It can happen. I mean, think about it. You and Maggie go out for dinner. You have a few drinks, some wine with dinner. You're tipsy, so you're not your sharpest. Then, when you're walking back to the parking lot when you least expect it–wham! Some punk jumps you, jams a gun right into your ribs and says he'll blow you to Kingdom Come if you don't do exactly what he says. Have you read the papers lately? There isn't a section in this city that that can't happen."

"I don't know if I want Mike answering that," Maggie says wrapping her arm around my shoulder.

"You don't have to answer that, Honey." She kisses my cheek.

"It's depressing," Cheryl says.

"I'll answer it," I say, grinding my butt into the ashtray. "I want to answer it. It's a good question. But first, I want to know what the guy did."

Joe laughs. He picks up his wine glass and swirls the liquid around. Then, he points it at me for accentuation.

"I can't tell you that until you answer."

Maggie's hand slips over mine. Her fingers burrow between my fingers and rest there. I can't help but imagine what her finger looked like with some other guy's diamond ring on it. I never met Darren, so I don't know what he's like. He could be a good guy or a real asshole. Maggie thinks the latter. I touch the top of her hand and she smiles. It must really feel like something to be engaged to a person. What, exactly, I couldn't say.

*****

"I'd fight him."

Joe's eyes light up. He has short, dark, wavy hair that never seems to cross beyond his hairline. He's about my size, maybe a little smaller, a good-natured fellow. He has thick wrists and short arms that would make him a hell of a tennis player, but a lousy boxer. No reach whatsoever. I've often watched Joe with a mixture of curiosity and intrigue and concluded with some certainty that I could take him in a fight.

"Be a hero, you mean?" he says.

"Save my wife," I say. Maggie knocks my knee with hers, and I'm immediately glad I'd said "wife" instead of "girlfriend." There's a certain entitlement in the distinction, a sense of worth. Darren never got the chance to say those words, or if he did, he doesn't anymore.

"But you're on the ground face-down. I mean, there's a small chance in hell that you're going to be able to get up and take away the gun from the kid without being shot or killed."

"At least I'd die trying."

"Michael!" Maggie says, slapping me on my arm.

"What? What did I say?"

"Why is it that men think that dying is so macho?" Maggie asks Cheryl.

"They watch too much John Wayne when they're younger. They see a man storm a fort or an Indian village and they think that's what it takes. Tell them, Maggie, women don't want heroes," Cheryl says. "If we did, I'd have married a Green Beret instead of an accountant."

"Sorry, boys, hate to burst your bubbles, but she's right—we don't want heroes," Maggie says.

Cheryl reaches for Joe, but he pushes her arm away from him.

"But you're all missing the point. It's not about bravery or lack of bravery. That's not the issue here. Mike says he'd fight the punk, but what he fails to see is that that doesn't help Maggie out any. The kid is going to rape her after he's shot. See, the question–the real question involved here–is not about courage or honor or any bullshit like that. What it's really about is forgiveness. Would you, Maggie, rather be raped and keep Mike alive and consequently have Mike living the rest of his life knowing that you were raped while he did nothing, or would Mike rather die trying to save Maggie like he said, knowing full well she's going to get raped after he's dead anyway?"

I light another cigarette. Maggie stares at the candle in the middle of the table. Cheryl rubs her face with her hand.

"Do you see what I'm saying?" Joe says.

*****

Through the sliding glass window that leads out to the terrace, I see a car pull into the parking space in front of the condo. A door opens and a woman gets out. She's around forty, dyed blonde hair with dark roots. She wears a lime green skirt suit. She looks like she's come home from work. She says something to her boyfriend or husband, whom I cannot see through the bushes, but I can hear the leather soles of their shoes clicking across the macadam–the dull clap of his wingtips and the high-pitched tick of her heels.

Joe looks back and forth between Maggie and me. A smirk rests on his face as he refills everyone's glasses with wine.

"One for the ages, isn't it?" he says. He grabs another cigarette from my pack.

"This is just silly," Cheryl remarks. "Why do you always bring up these impossible scenarios? Rape, murder, it's like living with Edgar Allen Poe."

"I disagree with you. There's nothing impossible about it," Joe says lifting the glass to his mouth. "It's a question of love. And trust. And forgiveness. And guilt. When you get right down to it, it's the human condition in a nutshell is what it is."

"I think you're drunk," Cheryl says.

"Of course I'm drunk. So is Mike. So is Maggie. That's what makes this interesting. Four drunk friends talking about life." He helps himself to another glass of wine.

"That's the last thing you need," Cheryl says pointing to the bottle with the burnt end of her smoke.

"There's plenty more where this came from. We can drink wine all night. We can drink wine until the sun comes up. *In vino veritas. Ergo est sum.*"

"Now I know he's drunk. Joe only spouts off Latin when he's half in the bag or stoned. He went to Catholic school, you know." Cheryl makes a crazy gesture, twirling a finger around her ear.

"Our Lady of Lourdes," he says proudly. "Our sports teams were called the Warriors. Have you ever heard of anything so ridiculous? Our Lady of Lourdes Warriors." He shakes his head. "Crazy," he says. "And let me just say, everything you hear about those nuns is fucking true."

"Joe!"

"Well, it is."

"You can't say 'nuns' and 'fucking' in the same sentence. It's got to be a sin, and if it isn't, it should be!"

"But it's true. How can it be sinful if it's true?"

Maggie, who's been quiet for some time, turns to me. She takes one of my hands and holds it in between both of hers. It's a genuine gesture and for a split-second, I know why I'm in love with her. "I know what I'd want to happen," Maggie says. "I could accept being raped knowing that Mike still lived. I mean that, Sweetheart. But what I couldn't handle is anything bad happening to you. That's not to say rape isn't bad, don't get me wrong, but it isn't death. It isn't forever."

"That's sweet," Cheryl says.

"I don't think many rape victims would agree with you on that," Joe counters. "In fact, I'm certain of that. What about you, Mike? Would you want Maggie to get raped just to save your measly life?"

"Shut up, Joe," I say.

*****

"See, what you've done? You've insulted our friends. God, I hate it when you get like this." Cheryl is angry. She steals another cigarette, but has trouble getting a match lit.

"I didn't mean anything by it," Joe says. "You know that, Mike. Hell, I love you guys. You're our best friends. I was just having fun, that's all."

"Sometimes you take fun over the limit," Cheryl says. She ruins two matches before getting the third one to ignite. The match head hisses into life.

"You've crossed the line again."

"I said I was sorry, didn't I? What can I do to make it up? Here, have a drink."

He pours the rest of the wine into my glass. He holds the bottle as the last drops plunk out.

"It's my fault, Joe," I say. "I got all tense. The wine makes me dizzy."

He puts his hands up to stop me.

"Hey, I know when I'm wrong. That's the best part of being married. Cheryl knows when I'm wrong and she isn't afraid to tell me whenever I've overstepped my right. That's when you know you've really got something special. When you can tell your significant other to go to hell and know that she still loves you for it. Isn't that right, Sweetie?"

He makes a funny face and nuzzles her neck.

"You're acting like a dickhead," she says, squirming in her seat. A smile tugs at the corners of her mouth as he continues to tickle her. She tries to fight it, but ends up cracking up instead.

"Dickhead?" he says with mock astonishment. "Dickhead? Would that be cut or uncut?" Joe attacks her sides with his fingers. Cheryl squirms some more in her chair.

"Enough!" she squeals, but she's laughing too hard for the demand to carry any weight. Her laughter is infectious. She sets off Maggie, and pretty soon, we're all in hysterics.

"Let's just forget about it," Maggie says finally.

"Let's talk about something else," Cheryl agrees, wiping the tears from her flushed face. She slugs Joe playfully in the arm and he feigns that it hurts.

"Ow," he says.

*****

"I've got a story," Maggie says.

We're all drunk now. Joe has brought out the hard stuff. In front of me, is a tall Jack and Coke, our favorite after dinner drink. Most people prefer cognac or some liqueur. I like something with a little more kick to it.

The fog in my head is thick. The women's eyes are glassy. I know Joe is pretty tight. He's still trying to smoke the filter.

"It's not going to get anyone upset, is it?" Joe says. He quickly glances over at his wife and puts his hand gently on her shoulder."Kidding, Honey."

"It might. It's a good story. I mean you want to talk about forgiveness, listen to this. It happened during Vietnam. During the war, I mean. One night, an army bus full of locals is going down the road to a nearby town." She pauses to take a sip of her wine. "Well, something happens as it always does. The driver has a heart attack and they run off the road into the bushes. It's pitch dark. In the distance, the people on board can hear a NVA patrol walking down the road. Everyone is terrified. This woman, young, maybe seventeen years old, her baby is crying. She can't quiet the baby. Now, everyone is getting pretty nervous. They can hear the patrol getting closer. But the woman, she just can't hush her child. People are shooting her dirty looks, pleading with her, begging her to keep the baby quiet. The woman doesn't know what to do. She's panicked. The jeeps are getting closer. You know how loud babies can be when they cry. If she can't still the baby, they are definitely going to be discovered. The patrol keeps getting closer. Now she's crying. The baby's crying. Everyone is whispering for her to shut the baby up. The tension is building. Then the patrol is upon them. It's walking right past them on the road. No one even dares breathe. All eyes are fixed on the mother who has her child pressed up against her, rocking back and forth, but nothing happens. The baby doesn't say a word. It's like a miracle. The patrol passes right on by without ever knowing they were there."

"They got lucky," Joe says. "It's a good thing she got that kid to shut the hell up."

Maggie looks at something on the floor. There is sad, distant expression on her face. She fiddles with a button on her shirt. I know I should touch her shoulder or something, but I don't.

"The mother suffocated her child," she says finally. "For the greater good, she murdered her own flesh and blood so that everyone would be spared. How about that for courage?"

Cheryl buries her head in her hands, the cigarette still wedged between her fingers. I watch the smoke curl in the space above the table.

After a long silence, Joe says matter-of-fact, "I could do that."

*****

Outside, a car horn beeps once or twice.

"Pizza guy," Joe says looking out the window. "Anyone order pizza?"

The rest of us groan.

The car drives around some, waits, leans on the horn once again, real long.

Cheryl puts on some Billie Holiday. Soon, the room is filled with her sorrowful voice. I've never felt so happy listening to something so sad. Cheryl sways to the music. "My parents gave us this for our wedding," she says meaning the stereo. "Can you believe it? What an odd gift for parents to give their child on her wedding day."

"Your mother is a kook, that's why I love her," Joe says. He puts an arm around Cheryl when she sits down and turns to us.

Maggie and I are holding hands beneath the table. We take turns trying to stick each other's fingernails in between the other person's fingernails.

"Her mother," he says. "You know her, Maggie, so you know what I'm saying. Kooky as the day is long."

"I don't think you met her at the wedding," Maggie says to me. "She's rather– eccentric."

"She's a kook, and I mean that in a good way. The best way possible."

"How long have they been married?" I ask when I feel like it's my turn to say something.

"Thirty years."

I rub my hand through my hair. Thirty years is an awful long time. A lot of water under the bridge as they say.

"Thirty years," I say. "That's something."

"You bet your ass it is," Joe says. "It's something to make it even half that nowadays. Divorce is for cowards."

"My mother always gives me strange gifts. Well, not strange exactly. Different. For my birthday one year, she gave me a violin and I didn't even know how to play."

"Maybe she wanted you to learn," Maggie says.

"No. I asked her about it. She said she always wanted a violin when she was my age, so she thought that I might like one. She's different that way. I don't know what you call it, but that's my mother." Cheryl smiles. She wraps her arm inside of Joe's. She nuzzles her face into his shoulder.

"My dad is the same way," Joe says. "I mean, you wouldn't know it if you saw him. Six-four, strong, decent body, Marine buzz cut. But when I was younger, like seven or eight, on weekends he'd tinker all day in the garage. That was his personal place, you know? His space, he called it. My mother was never allowed inside. He'd spend hours making the damndest things, and not one of them practical. Pencil holders shaped like boats and crap like that. For a while there, my mom actually thought he was a few bricks short of a load."

"What is it with parents," Maggie says. "Will we turn out the same way?"

"Not unless that boyfriend of yours slaps a ring on that finger," Joe says.

"Joe!" Cheryl slugs him on the arm. "Sorry," she says to me.

Maggie looks at me uncomfortably to see if my face registers any displeasure.

"What? He knows I'm kidding, right, Mike? You know I'm only kidding. I say shit all the time."

"I think we all turn into our parents in some fashion," Cheryl says. "It's inevitable. You spend most of your teens saying how much you're not going to be like them, then, one day, you're cutting coupons and thinking that a new set of drapes is more important than a weekend getaway."

"Amen to that," Maggie says.

"What about you, Mike? How about your father? Was he a whacko like the rest of them?"

I finish my Jack and coke and slam the glass down a little harder than I intended. It makes a loud noise that causes both women to jump.

"My dad died when I was a baby," I say.

Maggie squeezes my thigh.

Joe stares at the table. "Christ," he says.

\*\*\*\*\*

"Can you believe it? He's still out there." Joe walks from the window. "That's dedication for you. A pizza guy for the ages."

"We need more smokes," Maggie says crushing the soft pack in her hand.

"I'm too drunk to go anyplace," Cheryl says, putting her head on the table. "God, am I going to be hung-over tomorrow."

Joe walks out of the kitchen with the bottle of Jack Daniels and a couple of cans of coke.

"So what do you think? Another drink or what?"

"Not for me," Cheryl says.

Maggie groans. She gets up and settles herself into one of the comfortable chairs.

"Mike?" he asks.

I nod. Joe pours a healthy amount of Jack then a splash or two of coke. I listen to the fizz in the glass.

The women are tired. Cheryl rests her face on the table. Maggie is lying back with her eyes closed on the recliner.

"Looks like it's just us," he says, nodding to the two women.

"Just us," I say.

Joe leans in close. One hand is flat against the table, the other cups his glass. There is something in his eye, something on his mind.

"So what do you think? Really. Just between two guys. Two friends. Me and you."

"What do I think about what?"

"The question. What I asked you before. You know, about the situation. You still haven't answered me. What would you do?"

Maggie is sleeping. Her breath is heavy, thick. I don't have to see her to know how she is: Her head back, her mouth slightly open. It's a sound that's become very familiar to me, the way, I'm sure, it was familiar to Darren or any of the others, but it's an endearing sound. It's the sound of a person completely at rest.

"Well?"

I play with the ice in my drink.

Outside, the pizza guy makes another pass. I see his headlights between the dark shrubs, hear his engine as it goes around in circles. He drives around the complex, looking at the individual units, the small porch lights burning in the darkness. He makes a couple more passes, then leans on the horn once, long and hard, before he is gone.

## Pretty Things

That morning, Marla's mother took a turn for the worse. The call came in the morning. She had just broken two eggs and scrambled them for her younger brother, Scott. She cradled the phone between her shoulder and neck while she worked the frying pan. She moved the spatula around to keep the eggs from running into the bacon.

Doctor Struther was on the line. He specialized in the type of cancer that was killing her mother. It struck Marla odd at first–a specialist for a cancer where over seventy-percent of those afflicted, died. He informed her that the tests had returned from the lab and the prognosis wasn't good, but he also told her not to lose hope.

"Nothing's final," he said. "Remember that. There are still some things we can do."

Marla thanked the doctor and hung up the phone. Her hand lingered on the receiver. Then, she smelled something. The eggs were burning. She grabbed the handle.

"Son-of-a-bitch!" she screamed, dropping the frying pan into the sink. She sucked on her fingertips.

"Who was that on the phone?" Scott sat impassively at the table. If he didn't open his mouth from time to time, it would have been easy to forget about him. His face was pale, stony. She knew what was running around inside his head, and couldn't blame him for thinking that way. At eight, he had a better idea about death than most adults. Two years ago, their father had passed away in the same hospital their mother was at now. During those final days, when all that was really left was the waiting, Marla took Scott aside and explained what was going to happen. She didn't pull any punches; there wasn't talk of angels or souls or any of the conventional crap reserved for children. In this case, she believed that anything less than the truth was pure fiction, a placebo, easily swallowed, but offering no real comfort. Scott locked himself in his room the better part of that day. She heard him storm up and down, throw things against the wall, cry, but when he finally emerged, Marla noticed something different about her brother.

He had changed; his face possessed a survivor's edge.

Later, at the hospital, when they were notified of their father's death, neither child shed any tears.

"They're running more tests," she proclaimed pushing the eggs and bacon onto a plate. She set it down in front of him. He looked at the food a moment and made a face.

"I'm not hungry," he said.

"Eat it," she said. "You have to eat some-thing."

"What are you, deaf? I said I wasn't hungry."

"Look, don't give me any grief, okay? Just eat your food."

She pushed the plate closer to him, but he only shoved it back.

Her temper flared. Quit pushing me, Scott. I mean it."

"I'm not hungry, okay? You want me to eat it so bad, you eat it!"

Marla grabbed her brother's arm and twisted hard. The boy let out a scream, high-pitched, like a small animal caught in a trap. He tried to pull away, knocking over a juice glass, which spilled across the table and onto the floor.

"Look at what you did!" Her grip tightened.

"Let me go!"

"Brat!"

"Bitch!"

Scott wrenched his arm free. He got to his feet quickly, turning over his chair in the process. He ran toward the door, but slipped on the juice on the floor. His feet kicked out in front of him, his arms pin wheeling wildly, trying to find balance. He hung in the air a moment before he crashed to the floor his head hitting with a loud hollow smack.

"Scott!"

Marla reached out to touch the boy, but he pulled away from her. He stood slowly, rubbing his right elbow gingerly. There were red marks on his arm where her fingertips had been. She felt sick to her stomach. She opened her mouth to say something, but nothing came out. She sat down in the other chair and rubbed her head with both hands.

"What the hell is the matter with you?" he said.

*****

Scott boarded the faded yellow school bus. He turned and gave his sister a half-wave before the doors closed. Marla watched him walk down the aisle and select a seat near the window. He didn't look at her.

Some of the other kids were rambunctious, moving around in their seats, the pom-poms on their hats bouncing. The bus pulled away from the curb and lumbered down the street. Marla waited until it was out of sight before she turned to go back inside.

In the kitchen, she sat down at the table and lit a cigarette. The uneaten eggs remained on the plate.

She poked at their dull, lifeless form with a fork. Just like brains, she thought and then her stomach gave a violent jolt when she remembered her mother. She got up, retrieved her coffee, and took a sip. It was cold, but there was something else. Her hand trembled. She held it out in front of her and studied the shivering mug. Frustration gave way to anger, which gave way to fear. She shook more. The mug slipped from her fingers and crashed to the floor. Coffee and bits of ceramic splashed across the white linoleum mixing in with the juice already there. She lowered her face into her hands–the tears came now.

She cried for over an hour before she realized that today was her nineteenth birthday.

*****

Marla's fingers fired like pistons over the keys.

She liked to lose herself in the rhythm. There was no thought involved, just movement. It was as if her fingers were separate from her body, acting out their own volition, and as a result, the typing filled the room with its heavy sound.

She had already finished two letters for Mr. Bucci and was nearly done with a third. It was simple stuff to be sure, requesting additional inventory, filing bids, sending out invoices and late payment notices. She liked the work. The content wasn't important as was the volume. Mr. Bucci kept her busy and she was thankful for it.

Her morning job consisted mostly of secretarial and clerical duties for a small construction company. She answered phones, took down messages, filled Bucci's appointment book. She made coffee once when she got there in the morning, and once just after noon. The money she earned kept her brother fed and the utilities paid. If she had a choice, she would have preferred to be in school like the rest of her friends, but there was no choice.

"How's your mom doing?"

Marla looked up and saw Bucci leaning against the door frame. He was a short, dumpy man, whose large stomach required the use of both suspenders and a belt.

"She's fine. Stable." Then she added, "For now."

"That's good." He frowned. "She's going to get better."

"Sure she is. I know that."

There was a pause. Bucci brought a meaty hand to his chin and rubbed. He quickly averted his eyes from her when she looked at him. Marla felt the man's pity in the silence and immediately resented it. No matter how many times it happened, she just couldn't get accustomed to it–these odd moments when people felt compelled to say something, anything.

"That's some woman, your mother," he said. "I've known her since as long as I can remember. Since high school, can you believe that?"

"You've told me."

He frowned again. "Of course. I was just talking out loud." He looked down at his hands again, picking at the dirt in one nail. "I wouldn't worry about her, is all I was saying. That's one tough woman. If Betty Ryan is anything, it's tough. Take my word for it."

Marla said nothing. Bucci stood there as if waiting for her to respond. When she did not, he sighed, turned back into his office and closed the door. Marla resumed typing.

\*\*\*\*\*

At noon, she spent her lunch hour walking and smoking along the Merrimack River. She usually only took forty-five minutes, but Bucci urged her to take more if she needed it.

"I can manage around here," he said jokingly. "I know how to make my own coffee. Walk around some outside, clear your head. I don't even want to see you back much before two."

She thanked him and gathered her things.

Before she made it out the door, he added, "And for Chrissakes, get something to eat. I haven't seen you put two things in your mouth all week."

She nodded. He was right. The last thing she remembered eating was half a cupcake two days ago.

Truth was, she hadn't been hungry. Food had become something that other people needed. It was a weakness, a crutch, something for those who couldn't do without.

It was cold out, enough to wear a heavy sweater. It had rained the night before. The sky was still overcast, but showed signs of breaking in the East.

Marla moved slowly. She didn't even know how to begin to clear her head. There was so much to think about, so many possibilities. She walked the rest of Maple Court, which eventually ran into Post Road. From there she turned left, away from the center of town. She kept on this road past where the bronze monument for the fallen dead of World War II stood in a grassy rotary. There were a couple of small strip malls on both sides, but for the most part, the area was largely undeveloped. Two real estate agencies had set up shop and folded within a year of each other out here. One moment, there would be a new sign, the next, boarded-up windows. Every now and then, a car passed her. Sometimes, the driver would give her a quick burst on the horn before she realized she had drifted almost to the middle of the road.

She lit a new cigarette off the old one. She held the smoke in her lungs for as long as possible before expelling it. She repeated this two or three times, holding it a second longer than previous attempt.

Months before, she would have headed in the opposite direction; toward Scott's school and watched the kids play Four-Square at recess. She experienced a tremendous satisfaction back then, listening to the shrill, happy voices. Sometimes, especially when her mother had just started chemotherapy, Marla would stop by the hospital to visit her. She still had a full head of hair then, and still smiled despite vomiting occasionally from the radiation treatments.

Lately though, Marla's favorite place was the Unquowa Bridge, named for the Indians that had settled the area long ago. It was located on the far end of town, not too far from the offices of Bucci Construction. It was the main thoroughfare into or out of town. It loomed high up, a hundred feet or so, and was blackened from a century's worth of exhaust fumes and dirt. Beneath its steel frame, the Merrimack weaved down from one state and into another. In the springtime, when the weather was warmer, crew boats from the nearby university could be seen sculling in the early morning hours, fiberglass slivers that whisked by with the grace of water bugs.

Most people preferred the view from the bridge when the Black-eyed Susans and wild flowers bloomed along the banks and everything flourished in full color. Often, she had seen Mrs. Randolph setting up her easel on the walkway or several others vying for the best angle to snap a picture. Marla, on the other hand, liked the view from the bridge on clear nights when the river turned into a dark mirror for the stars above. When she looked at just the right angle, she could see the town lights reflected in the river's surface like a swarm of drunken fireflies.

Staring down at the water, Marla recalled the summer before her mother's illness. The three of them had watched the Fourth of July fireworks from the bridge. They lasted, she remembered, almost an entire hour. When the finale began, she leaned over the railing and watched the reflections of each Blooming Betty and Dazzling Stardust exploding in rapid-fire succession.

Standing there now, Marla replayed the events of that night. She recalled the loud bursts and the high-pitched shrills and the way Scott covered his ears with his hands.

Marla flicked her cigarette and watched it fall, the burnt end turning over on itself the entire way down.

"Lights," she said aloud to no one in particular.

*****

Bucci stopped by her desk on his way out. He put a large, pink hand on her calendar and she stared at his fat fingers. No matter how much picking he did, she noticed a thin ridge of dirt still rimmed the nails of his thumb and index fingers.

"She's going to be all right, you know."

"Sure she is. I know that."

"I'm not just saying this, you understand. I believe it. You have to believe it too. Not just say you do, but really do. It's important."

He paused to button his shirt cuff. "All kinds of things can happen, crazy things, miracles. You know, I once read somewhere that this old woman was diagnosed with leukemia. She went to all sorts of doctors and each one told her the same thing: Hopeless. But she kept a positive attitude. She fought it every step of the way. You know what happened? When she saw her doctor six months later, she was in complete remission. Damndest thing he said he ever saw."

He put his hand on top of hers. The gesture seemed more futile than reassuring. His hand was sweaty, soft. She looked at her own fingernails poking out from beneath the meaty mass. Faint chips of red polish lingered from when she last painted them a month ago.

"You're a pretty girl, Marla," he said finally. "It's a damn shame this had to happen, a damn shame."

She turned to him. 'Pretty' was a word she hadn't heard in a long time. She had been told this by her two previous boyfriends and her mother, of course, and now this man. At one time, she thought she might have been pretty too–at least, not bad looking–but in spite of everything, it just didn't seem right. Being pretty was just another useless burden, like sending flowers or sympathy cards, another thing to contend with.

Bucci lowered his eyes. He withdrew his hand and tapped on the calendar twice.

"I'm sorry," he said and headed for the door.

Before leaving he turned back to her. "I almost forgot. It's your birthday today, isn't it? Happy birthday."

\*\*\*\*\*

Marla hated the excursion down the sterile hallway. No matter how softly she walked, she heard her footsteps echo off the obscene white walls. From time to time, she passed a nurse who glanced up at her, then quickly averted her eyes. Marla could just imagine what went through the minds of these women when they saw someone like her walking aimlessly down this wing–another relative whose parent/aunt/uncle wouldn't survive another week, a month, a year.

She wrinkled her nose. The room smelled of disinfectant and death. It was a familiar odor, one that had steadily grown and taken over her father's room during his last days. There was no describing it, the sense of defeat, the relinquishment and exhaustion that presided here. She couldn't recall when it started or when she first noticed it. It just suddenly surfaced one day like a lesion, and she knew from past experience it would linger, even after the soul had passed, leaving the room steeped in a stale, sterilized unpleasantness. The only thing she could possibly equate it with was the smell emitted from a veterinarian's office–and her reaction, to that of a dog or cat affected by that horrible, invisible presence. The only difference separating then and now was that the cancer had infected the brain instead of the lung. Despite the fact that the experts disagreed over her mother's remaining time, they seemed fairly certain of the end result.

When her condition was downgraded to terminal, they moved her mother into a private room. There was a big battle with the insurance company. Several phone calls transpired between Marla and some faceless entity she knew only as "Mr. Lessing."

Threats of lawsuits and counter-suits were exchanged, but in the end, Marla had won out–a minor victory considering she still had to come up with money for an impending funeral.

*****

She paused before entering the room. A partition blocked most of her view. She saw only the lump of her mother's legs under the white blanket. Marla took a couple of deep breaths and straightened her blouse and skirt. She never knew what to say to her mother. Sometimes, Marla would tell her how Scott was doing. Other times, Marla stood there holding a cup in which the older woman spat up phlegm. On several occasions, her mother would be still, then suddenly burst into hysterics, refusing to calm down until she was sedated.

Thankfully, she found her mother asleep, or else doped up on one medication or another. They all seemed the same: Codeine, morphine, whatever did the best to numb the pain. They gave her several different pills of varying sizes and colors. Once, when it was really bad, a doctor administered a shot.

Marla studied her mother's sleeping form–her head was nearly bald with only a few wisps of hair. Her cheeks were so deeply lined that when relaxed as they were now, sagged like the wrinkled skin of a peach. She wanted to touch her mother, but couldn't. Her fingers stretched out but retracted slowly. Instead, Marla touched her own face, running her fingertips all over–her cheekbones, her eyes, her nose, her lips.

Then, a thought struck her. Had her mother ever been pretty? She had never given this much thought before and she definitely couldn't tell now.

This body, this form in front of her, was only a fraction of who her mother had been. What about a time prior to this terminal condition? Before marriage and two kids, and a mortgage only half-paid? Had she been pretty then? Marla racked her brain, but couldn't recall a single incident when her father had referred to his wife by anything else but her name.

Sure, he had said "dear" and "swee-theart" (endearing terms not affectionate ones, she noted) whenever he wanted something, but never once did she hear him call her "beautiful" or "sexy" or least of all, "pretty."

Looking at her now, there was no misinterpreting her mother for anything but what she was, a faceless, dying woman.

Marla dipped her hand into her bag and retrieved a brown compact. Leaning over the bed, she applied powder onto her mother's sallow features. She patted carefully, working it in between the deep wrinkles. The skin was extremely loose in areas, as if it had been a size too large. It felt foreign to the touch like latex: Almost real, but not quite.

She paused a moment and recon-sidered her subject. She removed another small case and opened the rouge. She worked hard, adding and subtracting the bright color with the side of her hand. Now and then, she stopped to brush away the hair that fell over her eyes. When she was finished, Marla stepped back to appraise her efforts. The pale complexion had been replaced with a healthy, albeit artificial, glow.

"I'm sorry, but you're going to have to come back tomorrow. Visiting hours are over."

"Of course, I didn't mean to stay so long."

"Hey, no problem, I just have some things I have to do for her that you can't be here for: Hospital rules. You understand."

Marla nodded.

The nurse wheeled in a cart loaded with various instruments and containers. There were things on it that she had never seen before, things that made her stomach jump. Marla turned away from the nurse and looked out the window. It was steadily darkening outside, but clear just as the weather report promised. Marla got her things together.

The nurse checked the machines, then pressed her fingers against Marla's mother's wrist and looked at her watch.

"You do this?" the nurse asked, looking at the patient. "She looks good."

Marla shrugged. She wanted to tell this woman everything, but didn't know where or how to begin.

"It's something. I mean–you know."

The nurse made a notation on a chart. "I know, Honey," she said. "Believe me, I know."

*****

The Sweet Shop had been closed for over an hour. There wasn't much business for ice cream in late fall past six o'clock. In another week or so, the shop would close up until spring, and she would be shit-out-of-luck. She knew that she needed to find another part time job, and soon. She considered waitressing at Stucky's or one of the late-night diners across the way. In any case, something had to be done. Too many bills found their way under her door lately, demanding partial payment. The last two had been sent certified.

Marla stopped to catch her breath. She leaned the mop against the counter and buried her head into her hands. She rubbed her temples with her fingers.

Scott was at Joey Swenson's house. That was an arrangement she made when the doctors put her mother on hospice. The Swensons–Sylvia and Joe, Sr.– were all too happy to help. They understood her situation, they told her. Scott was welcome to stay with them all the time if she wanted, not just after school. He was like one of their own. Her mother would do the same for them if the situations were reversed. Who wouldn't?

Marla lit a cigarette. Everyone seemed too willing to share in each other's tragedy and happiness.

It was like the town strengthened its identity by pitching-in whenever it could, attending weddings, burying the dead.

Later, she would pick up Scott and they would drive home together. In the car, he would rattle on about how normal the Swensons were, as he did every night, and how nothing bad ever happened to them, and Marla would drive quietly, listening with the strained patience of someone who recognized that her life was not going how she originally intended.

*****

She dialed the phone. She chewed on a thumbnail as it rang. She lit another cigarette and watched her fingers tremble with the match. The flame went out. She lit another one, inhaled, and blew out the smoke. After the fourth ring, Mr. Swenson picked up.

"Hello?"

"Mr. Swenson? It's Marla."

Her voice was strong. Even she amazed at how well she sounded.

"Marla. How are you? Is everything all right?"

"Everything's fine Mr. Swenson, something's come up is all. I may be a little late tonight."

There was a pause. She could hear Mrs. Swenson ask her husband something. Then, Mr. Swenson came back. "Are you sure everything is okay? You don't sound okay. How is your mother doing?"

"The same. Listen," she said, "I was wondering, do you think–I mean, would it be all right if Scott spent the night tonight?"

"Yes, of course it's fine. It's more than fine. Scott is welcome here any time. So are you. You know that. Why don't I come and pick you up? Where are you?"

"No really, I'm okay; I'm just mopping the floors at the Sweet Shop. It's taking longer than I expected. Mr. Swenson? I just wanted to say, thanks. For Scott. I really appreciate this."

"Don't be silly. Look, I could be there in ten minutes."

"No, I'm not done yet. Maybe tomorrow though."

Mr. Swenson said something else, but Marla just hung up the phone.

Later, she returned the mop to the supply closet. She removed her apron and hung it up on the door, then stared at her reflection in the dirty mirror. She reached out for the face staring back at her, but stopped before her fingers touched the glass. Instead, she turned them on herself again, touching the soft, dark area beneath her eyes, running them along her forehead, her chin. She bent her nose side to side, opened her mouth, stuck out her tongue. She pulled back hard on her cheeks until it hurt.

The whole time, one thing kept playing over and over in her head: *I should be in college now.*

She spotted the disposable razor on the side of the sink. How curious it looked, so out of place in this setting. It was plastic, cheap, the kind that came in a package of five for ninety-nine cents. She picked it up and studied it in the dim light. She tested the blade with the meat of one thumb, jerking back as blood speckled the white sink.

Marla stared at the mirror again, keeping eye contact with her image. She took a deep breath, running the edge of the razor down one cheek. She didn't even feel it split her skin, not even when the blood surfaced and oozed down her face. Then she ran the blade down the other side. She didn't hesitate. Not once did she think twice as her eyes remained focused on her gruesome reflection.

Was she pretty now?

\*\*\*\*\*

On the bridge, Marla looked down at the river. It was cold out; the wind blew past her face sending her dark hair trailing behind her like a scarf. Her cuts throbbed in the breeze. She wondered how she must look with two deep gashes–one for each awful turn in her life–down her once lovely face.

She shifted her attention back to the lights on the water. They still shimmered like drunk fireflies. She turned her head this way and that, and they turned with her, like the eyes of a painting that follow a person around a room.

Somewhere, maybe in her mind, explosions went off: bright, colorful explosions. She smiled. Marla climbed the metal side, working her fingers into the tight nooks, pulling herself up until her feet rested on top of the railing. She grabbed the support cable for balance. She swayed in the wind, her skirt rippling.

"Happy birthday!" her voice rang out. It hung in the air an instant before dissipating in the space around her.

Behind her, a couple of cars passed. One or two leaned on their horns and the driver of a third screamed out his window, "You crazy, bitch!"

Marla stepped from the railing. The air rushed past her swollen face.

She fell.
She kept on falling.

## What Are You Looking At?

Zeke decides to come out when he sees me in the driveway. I spot him through the picture window of his ranch home putting on his hat and scarf, his wife helping him shrug into the red hunting coat she bought him last winter. He sinks half-way down beneath the sill to pull on his boots–first left, then right. Moments later, he meets me out in the snow. I smell his cigar long before I even hear his screen door whine shut. They're pharmacy specials: White Owl Invincibles, ten for two bucks. They carry a pungent odor, just like Zeke.

"Hey Bill," he says inspecting the path I've made with my shovel. "Hell of a storm last night."

"Yeah," I wheeze tossing aside a shovel-full of slush. "Bitch is heavy too."

"Wet snow," he puffs, "Worst kind."

"Worst kind," I repeat, turning my back on him.

Zeke is a few years older than me, with a full stock of hair that suddenly turned white one day for no explicable reason. His most startling feature is his nose, which looks like someone had slammed the door on it without realizing he was there. Standing in the light as he does, he looks sixty-five instead of fifty. His wife, Marge, is a few years younger than him and one hell of a baker. We've lived next to one another for the past ten years, feasting on the French apple pies and Dutch coffee cakes from her oven. About this time, Helen and I usually find oatmeal raisin cookies and fruit cake on our doorstep with a note shaped into a reindeer or a wreath proclaiming From our house to yours, with warm wishes, the Hendersons. This year, we didn't find a thing.

"Last night me and the missus sat by the fire watching it all come down. Sometimes, we couldn't even see the flakes it was coming down so hard. Like one big sheet of white."

I grunt something unintelligible back. He takes a sweeping view of the street. Strips of windshields peer out like periscopes from beneath the worst snowfall in thirty years. We both listen to Jewel Miller's kids shouting from their yard across the street. Two kids, a boy and a girl, rough-house in the thick drifts.

"Did you notice the damn plow didn't come down here once," he says gruffly.

"I know. I listened for it. What do I pay county taxes for if they aren't going to plow? They think just because they send a truck down here, they did their job. Not in my book. No sir. You got to actually lower the plow to make it count. That's plowing. None of this drive down the street shit to make grooves for the tires."

Zeke chews on his Invincible. He's offered me one on several occasions, but I only accepted once, at last year's Christmas party. It was right before everyone went out and played in the snow. Drunk grownups threw snowballs at one another or rubbed snow angels into the ground. It was really something. Me and Zeke watched the whole thing, smoking our Invincibles. It doesn't take too much effort to recall that bitter taste on my tongue if you know what I mean.

I continue shoveling, trying not to put my back into it so much. During the news last night, they demonstrated the right ways and wrong ways to shovel snow. More legs, less back, that's what they said. I've been doing the reverse all my life, but that's the way it is with our society. They tell you one thing one year, then something else the next. They did the same thing with saccharin, remember? First it was the miracle sweetener; then it caused cancer. Just watch, next thing you know, they'll be saying that the best way to shovel is with your back and not your legs; save wear and tear on your knees or something crazy like that.

"Eighteen inches...who would have thought so much snow could pile up at one time down here?" More puffing. "Hell, that's why I moved south in the first place. Got tired of seeing the damn snow everyplace. Snow wasn't a weather condition in Syracuse, it was a season." He pauses to blow more smoke. "Guess I should bust out a shovel soon myself," he says.

But Zeke doesn't move. He keeps chewing on his cigar, waiting for me to say something.

*****

This time last year, the Hendersons hosted their yearly open house for the neighborhood. It was a small holiday gathering of sorts, adults only. They decorated the house in the usual fanfare: Flashy red and green garland bordered the windows and wrapped around the base of a small, but plump Christmas tree. Nat King Cole crooned on the stereo. Mistletoe surprised guests in the foyer, embarrassing loved ones to kiss awkwardly in the name of holiday cheer. It was a good party, plenty of booze and food. Everyone got toasted. Zeke dressed up like Saint Nick and handed out his customary gag gifts to everybody, silly string and squirting flowers, things like that. I got a novelty ceramic Yuletide mug. Marge made a big spread of dips, chips, cheese and crackers, and Virginia honey baked ham. She even broke out her Christmas candlesticks, heirlooms from some great aunt or other who had passed them down her family line. They were hand crafted out of solid silver and shaped like angels, their innocent heads bowed in silent prayer. They had long, graceful wings and slender hands that came together to form a circle through which the candles were stuck. They were pretty impressive as far as candlesticks went.

It snowed a second time later that evening. Elaine McCabe went out first on a dare. She and her husband, Mel, started to make a snowman. It looked like fun, so the Bernsteins followed, then the Stewarts. Pretty soon, darn near everyone was out there, throwing snowballs and laughing. All of these stumbling adults were rolling in the snow, white-washing each other while their children slept in houses across the street and down the block. It was really something. That's when me and Zeke smoked the cigars, watching Jewel Miller fall flat on her back, moving her arms and legs back and forth, to make a snow angel.

The next day though, Marge discovered one of her candlesticks was missing. She went into a tizzy. I mean she ransacked her house from top to bottom, bottom to top and back again. She tore through every square inch of that place. They were invaluable, those candlesticks. She told us that every year. Losing one was like losing a child, not that she had any. That's when all hell broke loose. I don't know how she pegged my wife for the crime, but sure enough, she stormed right over, dragging old Zeke along. I remember. Helen and I were working on our second cups of coffee when Marge barged right in without even knocking.

"Where is it?! Where is it?!" she demanded.

"Marge?" I asked, then saw her march right into our kitchen with Zeke in tow. "What is it? What's wrong?"

"Don't give me this 'what's wrong' crap! Where's my damn angel?"

"Your what?" Helen asked, putting down her section of the paper.

"You know damn well what I'm talking about, Helen! I saw you eyeballing it! You and Gail were hanging around the table all night! Now, I want it back!"

"Hold on," I said, getting to my feet. My head throbbed from the hangover and made everything hazy when I moved too fast. "Before you start accusing anybody of anything, what's going on?"

Zeke scratched behind his ear. He looked down at the white space on the floor where a tile used to be. He stared long and hard at that empty space, avoiding any eye contact.

"One of Margie's candlesticks is missing," he said almost apologetically. "I told her maybe someone took it as a joke or something, since only one was taken."

"If it's a joke, it's certainly in poor taste!" Marge said huffily.

"Look, I'm terribly sorry," Helen said, "but you're mistaken. I didn't take them. I don't know who would do such a thing."

"I saw the way you were looking at them! Every year you look at them that way. Don't think I haven't noticed, because I have."

"I do like them. But I didn't take it. I wouldn't do that."

"Like hell you wouldn't!" snapped Marge.

"Maybe we should sit down," I offered, my temper rising. My head was killing me. "Let's all sit down and have some coffee and talk this out rationally."

"Thanks all the same," Zeke said. His finger found his ear again. "But I got to say–and this pains me to say it, Bill, I want you to know that–but I saw Helen pick the thing up when no one was around. Kind of looking at it, if you know what I mean."

Helen's mouth formed a hollow "O" as a cry of indignation escaped her. "I was looking at it for crying out loud, Zeke, but I didn't take it!"

"Quite frankly, Helen," Marge said icily. "I don't believe you."

"You have to be kidding me," said Helen. She looked at me briefly. I shrugged. The whole thing was crazy.

"Even if I did take it," she continued, "why would I want just one? Tell me that. I mean, it just doesn't make sense. What good would one candlestick do?"

"That's why I thought that maybe you did it as a joke or something," Zeke offered.

"My wife doesn't make jokes like that," I snapped at Zeke. He looked at me for a moment, then back to the space in the tile again. This time, I resented him looking at it that way, like it was yet another bit of evidence to hold against us.

"I want it back or I'm calling the cops," Marge threatened.

"Call them," Helen said. She grabbed the cordless phone off the wall. "I'll even dial the phone for you. They can search this whole fucking house for all I care."

The women glared at each other like two stray cats in an alley. The hairs on my neck stood on end. I'd seen that look on Helen only one other time: When she punched an old priest in the face for calling her support of Pro-Choice "abominable."

"Come on, Zeke," she said finally, tugging her husband's arm. "This is leading to no good."

Zeke looked at me briefly, then turned for the door.

That was the last time we spoke to each other for an entire year.

She found the candlestick later that night in the sofa cushions.

*****

Nothing was the same anymore between us. Helen threw out the fruitcake Marge had baked for her and left on the doorstep as an apology. She didn't even unwrap the foil, just threw it out without a word, without any sign of emotion. When we went out, she drove right by them, never acknowledging their waves or smiles. In fact, she showed no recognition of them whatsoever. It was as if they were as meaningless and immaterial as porcelain figurines on a mantel. She didn't return any of Marge's phone calls. I never saw Helen so pissed, not that I blamed her. Trust was like anything else made cheaply; too easily broken, too impossible to mend.

\*\*\*\*\*

This falling out stretched to Zeke and me, as well as Zeke and Helen, and finally Marge and me. A wall of silence was erected between our properties. We didn't look at them and they didn't look at us, at least most of the time, they didn't. When winter turned to spring, any tiny hope the Hendersons had in the way of reconciliation was instantly crushed when Helen tore up their letter at the mailbox, sprinkling the pieces over their driveway. By the time summer came around, they had accepted the inevitable. I watered my lawn or weeded the beds only when I was sure that Zeke wasn't out or else had already finished his yard work. No invitations were extended to the Hendersons for our weekly barbecues, and they never offered us the services of their pool, even when the humidity reached a hundred and ten percent.

No one said anything to anyone.

\*\*\*\*\*

Zeke kicks some snow around with his boot.

Across the street, Jewel's two kids scream happily, a snow fight, or else the boy is teasing his sister. I see them running around the house, the pom-poms of their hats bouncing, their blue and pink nylon snowsuits swishing.

I plant my shovel deep and lift for all I'm worth. It's heavy, but I don't want to show any signs of stopping, that I can stop. He fills his mouth with smoke, then releases it in dribbles. It blows past his face and disappears somewhere over his property.

"We're not having the party this year," he says as a matter of fact. "Just aren't into the spirit, I guess."

"Happens," I grunt. In all this time, our eyes haven't met. I'm not sure if I'm proud of that fact or not.

"Yeah, I guess it does at that. Especially with all this snow around. It's going to take half the winter just for this stuff to melt."

He chuckles to himself uncomfortably. I can feel his eyes following the path of my shovel: Plunge, lift, toss, plunge, lift, toss. He's with me every step of the way.

"I guess it does at that," he says again, and this time, I hear the sadness in his voice.

He starts to drift away from me, backing slowly, not really wanting to, but understanding that the choice isn't his. "Don't strain yourself out here, Bill," he says, retreating a little bit further. "It's not good for the ticker."

I raise a hand in acknowledgment, but still don't look up. I pretend to concentrate on my shoveling until I hear his screen door whine and slam shut. Then, I stand up straight, stretching out my back.

The kids return to the front of the house now. They're young, six and seven respectively, Jeff Jr. and Mattie. They throw snow at one another, their voices tearing through the cold air, first a scream, then laughter. She scoops up small handfuls and tosses them at her brother. He makes a snowball and hits her on the back. She takes off and he chases her around the house.

Helen pops her head out the door. "Coffee," she says, holding out a steaming mug that has a cartoon of these bizarre individuals with crazy expressions on their faces. They're at this party and each person is doing something more ridiculous than someone else. The caption beneath it reads, "Joy to the Weird."

The girl comes around front, then suddenly drops on her back, and rapidly rubs her arms and legs into the snow. Moments later, Jeff Jr. spots his sister, plops down and does the same. Side-by-side they lay, limbs moving, voices cackling with laughter.

I walk over to Helen and take the mug. The coffee's good and hot, light, with a hint of sugar, just the way I like it. It warms my fingers through the tattered gloves.

"What did he want?" she asks, meaning Zeke.

"Nothing," I say, "just wanted to know what I thought about all this."

"He's got some nerve," she says stiffly. She blows air into her palms and rubs them together. She keeps at it. She's relentless that way. "I want nothing to do with those people. Nothing at all."

The kids are gone now. Their mother called them in. She opened the door and I heard her tell them to take off their boots before they walked over the floor. Jewell looked at me and Helen. It was just a look, but some looks are more telling than others.

"What are you looking at? Bill? Are you listening to me? What is it, Darling?"

I don't move. I keep standing there, my eyes squinting in the glare. There's something there, something I can't quite make out in the snow. Imprints of some kind, blurred impressions, shapes, almost formless.

"Bill?"

I turn to face her but only one word croaks out.

She makes a face. She doesn't understand.

I don't blame her. It doesn't make much sense unless you know what it means, unless you know where it's coming from. That's when I point. I stick my hand straight out and it shakes in the cold.

"Look," I tell her. "Wings."

## Hair of the Dog

I can't sleep. My back isn't right. It hurts in the middle, right near the spine. It also hurts in the same area a little lower down. It's like someone gave me a good kick in the kidneys. It reminds me of when I was drinking and I'd wake up covered with bruises from God knows what. It hurts that much. I try rolling on one side then the other, but neither does any good. I still can't get comfortable, and I need to sleep. Tomorrow, my brother is coming to stay with us for a little while. That's what he said, "A little while."

The girl he was living with left him, or he left her, I don't remember. I can't really keep up with the numbers anymore. Just when you got one face down the next month, a new one surfaces. He's lived with more women than I can count--and names–my God, don't even go there. During Thanksgiving one year, he nearly drove our poor mother nuts because the girl he was seeing and the one before her were both named Megan, except one pronounced it "Mee-gan" and the other "Me-gan." Needless to say, it caused an embarrassing, if not comical, situation.

Right now, though, it's my back that worries me, not my brother. Every time I move, my shoulders and spine are in agony. I turn over again, but it's no use. The pain is constant like a toothache, only more severe. Finally, I give up and get out of bed. I reach around and try to touch the sore areas with my fingers.

"Jesus," I say.

Marion turns on the light. She sits up and adjusts her pillow behind her so that she can lean against the headboard. Her eyes are half-closed and she shields her face with her hands until her eyes adjust to the brightness. She's been sleeping fine, but she's always been that way.

"What's the matter, Honey?"

"My back," I tell her.

"Still?"

My back has been hurting for the past two days. I really can't explain it. I haven't worked out or done any heavy lifting. I've retraced every step I've made since Friday and still can't come up with anything that might cause pain like this.

"No, I'm thinking about using this for a comedy routine," I say and feel immediately sorry for saying it. "I didn't mean that the way it sounded."

"Have you tried lying on the floor? The floor is supposed to be good for your back. Straighten out your spine. My grandmother slept on a board most her life because of her back troubles."

"That's a good idea."

I get down on the floor near my side of the bed. First, I try stretching completely out, and then bend both knees. I concentrate on pushing my lower back to the floor. Marion leans her head over the side. There's a line running down her cheek where the pillow case has left its imprint.

"Well?

I shake my head. "Nope. It's no good. I can still feel it. Pain, right here and here." I turn over and point to the troubled spots.

"Maybe some aspirin will help."

Marion climbs over me and walks to the bathroom barefoot. I see her in the doorway opening the medicine cabinet. She rattles around a couple of bottles. I look over at the clock and groan when I see the time. I really need to sleep. Tomorrow is going to be a long day. I have to help my brother move his stuff into the basement–his stereo equipment, his futon bed, and that fold-up exercise contraption, the kind that supposedly works out every muscle group. I think he mentioned a loveseat somewhere in there and some other things. He gave me the list earlier tonight on the phone.

"Hope you been hitting the weights," he said. His voice was upbeat, happy. Why shouldn't it be? He was playing sleep-away at my expense. Once, during an all-night drink-fest, he told me that the reason he never foresaw himself getting married was because it would take too long to sort out the "whose things are whose" scenario. He got short-changed a couple of years back by this ski instructor in New Mexico and swore it'd be a cold day in hell before that ever happened again.

"This way, what's mine is mine, and what's hers is hers," is how he put it. He said he put little tags on his things just to make sure. Of course, my brother has little to complain about. As long as I've known him, he has never paid a mortgage or a steady rent for that matter. He is a man without purpose. He goes through life like he goes through girls.

*****

"Aspirin or Ibuprofen?" Marion asks.

"What?"

"Aspirin or Ibuprofen? We have both."

"Jesus, I don't know. Whichever works best."

She has a bottle in each hand as if weighing the merit of both. She reads the back of one, then the other, then opens the cap on the first one. She turns on the tap and fills a glass.

"I think aspirin is better. Ibuprofen is more for a fever. You have a fever?"

"No."

Marion isn't happy that he's coming and I don't blame her. Kyle is a wild card. He wavers somewhere between being a liability and a loose cannon. I should know, I used to be the same way. I had a thing for the bottle, just like Kyle has, and when you put us together, man, we did some crazy stuff. I eventually got help, even if the program didn't take until the third time trying. My live-in girlfriend, Stacy, couldn't deal with me then. I was never in my right mind. It was a different time, an "I don't care" era, if you will. There's a lot of empty space in that era, complete chunks of time I can't even remember. Kyle and I used to go out to all hours. Usually, we went to our local bar, but it didn't have to be a local bar. Sometimes, we'd swing by one of the university hangouts or a real dive and try to stir up trouble. We'd get into fights with bikers, or college kids, or mill workers–whoever was as drunk and stupid as we were. There were some real rough moments. Sometimes, we'd win, but most of the time, we didn't. I woke up twice in the hospital without ever knowing how I got there. I've had cracked ribs and my nose busted up a couple of times, but Kyle was worse. He's woken up in other states before, most of the time without his wallet, keys, or, on one occasion, half of his clothes. But that's all in the past. I don't do that anymore. It took Stacy leaving me before I understood that I wasn't going anywhere living like that. I wish I could say that my drinking stopped, but as I said before, the third time was the charm.

*****

"Try these." Marion hands me the aspirin. I look at the small, white pills and pop them into my mouth without a second thought. When I was boozed up, I didn't trust anybody, least of all, my brother. It's amazing how much trust I have in her, how much we have in each other. It goes to show how far I've come since then. For all intents and purposes, Marion could have easily slipped me arsenic or cyanide and I just took them like that, like they were candy. I tell her this and she laughs.

"Sure, so I can inherit all that money you have."

It's so funny that I laugh with her and, for a few moments, our laughter fills the still room. It's a nice strong sound. It fades quickly as she sits on the bed next to me and puts her hands on my shoulders.

"What are we going to do?" she asks.

"What do you mean?"

"Nothing. Forget I said anything. You want a massage? That might do the trick, a nice backrub."

I tell her that sounds good. I mean, I'm not getting to sleep anytime in the near future, not with pain like this. Who knows? Maybe this is the very thing I need. She starts rubbing. Her fingers are strong.

She's been hardened from years of carrying trays of cocktails, and I don't mean just the calluses on her fingers. She kneads my shoulder blades, really working the flesh.

"You're all knots," she says.

"I'm stressed."

"Then what are you having him stay here for? Can I ask that? What purpose does it serve?"

"Let's not get into this again."

She works her fingers gradually down my spine. She's careful, making sure she doesn't miss anything. When she hits the right spots, I squirm a little and groan.

"Did I hurt you? Is that the spot?"

"That's one," I manage. "There's another lower down."

She pauses to crack her knuckles and exhales loudly. It's her nervous habit, what she does when she doesn't know what to say. She takes just long enough to think of something, and then she sets her fingers to work again.

"Look, Ray, I'm not trying to get into it again, okay? I'm just asking. I have that right. I know he's your brother, but he's got a bad effect on you. I mean, Christ, look at you. You're all tense. You see what I'm saying here, Hon?"

She's concerned and rightly so. She knows all the stories. I've kept nothing from her like I did from Stacy. You make the same mistake enough times, it's bound to sink in sooner or later, right? To be honest, I'm lucky to have Marion. She knows the score. She's been a waitress and a drunk most of her adult life– sneaking nips now and then, finishing the glasses left by other people. I don't know what set her straight, to this day, she won't tell me about it, even though I think it has something to do with the scar down her left breast. There's always a defining incident in a drunk's life that either saves her or kills her, and it usually isn't pretty. But Marion's tough as nails. Whatever that moment was, it's kept her sober five years and counting.

When we first got together, I asked her why she still worked as a cocktail waitress, being in recovery and all.

"Because I won't let it beat me," she said. "I've worked too hard, done too much to have a state of momentary weakness. Working at the bar keeps me straight. It makes me remember the bad times."

I know the way a former drunk looks at a bottle–it's always a possibility, a temptation: One more thing you can't have. She's a strong person; much stronger than I am, God knows. That's why we're perfect for each other. I don't have to tell her the way it is, she's already been there. What a sight we are, two former drunks trying to make something of the remaining parts of our lives.

By that same token, she doesn't have much patience for this sort of thing. That's why she knows my brother's no good. She knows what he represents.

She recognizes the signs. She calls him a tornado drunk; uncontrollable, too willing to take down other people in his path.

Two years ago, the year my mother got sick, Kyle disappeared for six months. No one heard from him, no one knew whether he was alive or dead. I had just been released from Hillcrest, the drying-out facility upstate. It was my third time in as many years. They had seen me so often that by this time that all the volunteers knew me by name. They even let me have my old room back on the second floor and returned all of my favorite magazines. In the sessions, the counselors told me that I'd have to be strong. I'd have to find it within myself to stop or else it'd stop me. I couldn't help but wonder if they had my brother Kyle in mind when they said that, but alcohol is a strange potion. It's not like a few months can really erase a lifetime of familiarity. That's why there are setbacks.

On my way out, they gave me a physical. That's when the doctors told me another relapse might do me in. By this time, Stacy had already sent me the letter–she couldn't take it anymore. She was leaving me, taking her things, moving back out West, so there was no one to pick me up. I had to take a bus back home. It was a sad sight, pulling into the station, seeing the pollution, the gray sky, the sagging buildings. It's always a struggle to return to a place that holds nothing but bad memories. I don't mind telling you I was like a foal on shaky legs.

Then, about a week after I'd settled into my place, I got this call from my mother's landlady. She told me that she had found my mother on the bathroom floor, pitching fits. She had taken her to the hospital where they told her that my mother had suffered a severe stroke. Well, that was the last thing I needed. Instead of getting a handle on things and trying to put my life back together, I spent those first few days with my mother, staring at her pale body, wishing I was anyplace else. When I wasn't thinking about my mother, I was worrying about Kyle. It wasn't unusual for him to just pick up and go someplace, but he always found his way back, no matter what, just like a homing pigeon. Whenever the phone rang at night, I half-expected to hear some cop's voice telling me where I could come claim Kyle's body. I was a complete wreck. I was sober, vulnerable, jittery. I couldn't sleep. Hell, I'll say it, I needed a drink.

The night the doctors told me my mother wouldn't last the week, I found myself sitting at the bar of the Blarney Stone. I had already ordered a bourbon and soda, collected my change. I hadn't taken a sip of it yet. I was just looking at it, watching the beads of sweat run down the sides of the glass. I don't remember what was going through my mind, but I know I was afraid, that much I'm certain. The mere thought of alcohol then scared the hell out of me. I wanted to touch the glass, but couldn't muster the courage. My fingers got close, but that's about it. Visions of my mother's face, the counselor's face, my brother's broken body lying in some train yard somewhere, completely overwhelmed me. And that's when it all fell apart. I started crying, can you believe it? There I was, a full-grown man, a drunk, bawling his eyes out in the middle of a bar for no Goddamn reason.

It was some sight, I tell you.

That's when Marion appeared, my little angel of mercy. She must have seen me from across the room or something, I don't know, but I had completely lost it. I had reached my breaking point. I needed to be rescued or else it was over. And that's what she did.

She put down her tray and wrapped her arms around me and I cried into her soft bosom.

"It's okay, Honey. Get it all out," she said, stroking my hair.

From then on, I knew things had to get better because they sure as hell couldn't get much worse.

*****

My first girl, Stacy, was a nurse's assistant. If she were here, she would say that my ailing back was psychosomatic. She was always telling me that.

"Most of your problems," she said to me once, "are all in your head."

There was this once incident in particular that stands out. I'm not proud of it, but I have to tell it. I had gone back to the bottle two months after my second stay at Hillcrest. I had been good for a while, but a beer or two watching the ball game quickly escalated into a scotch or two. Things have a way of snowballing. For some reason, I was pretty convinced I had a brain tumor. My head was killing me, not like my back is now, but close to it. There were these little ripples of pain I felt on one side of my skull that when they got going, nearly blinded me. It was sometime late afternoon. Stacy had just gotten off her shift. I had been drinking bourbon for an hour to numb the pain and it wasn't working.

"I think I'm dying," I told her.

"You're not dying, you just have a headache. You might have a migraine, but I doubt it." She was reading a magazine on the sofa. She wasn't really paying attention to me, which was pissing me off. She was still in her white nurse's uniform although she had removed her shoes. One leg dangled over the armrest.

"I'm serious. My head." I stumbled to her, tripping over a tear in the carpet. It's safe to say I was a bit drunk by this point. I fell to my knees and spilled my drink over the front of my shirt. "Goddamn it," I said. "Would you just check it out for me, please?"

She sighed and put down her magazine. She was tired, I'm sure, although I wouldn't have recognized it then.

"You aren't dying. You stayed out too late with that loser brother of yours. You're off the wagon again. You haven't eaten more than peanuts in the past two days. And you wonder why you have a headache?"

"Come on," I pleaded. I lowered my head to her. I pointed to the spot. "Right there. Go on. Touch it. Tell me I don't have a tumor."

She touched me, but she wasn't serious. She kind of ran her fingers around my hair a little; that was all.

"You're fine," she said. "Jesus, Ray, I see people every day–car accidents, stabbings, burn victims–who wish they were in your condition. So excuse me for not getting all excited over a stupid headache."

I'm not quite sure what happened then. Maybe it was what she said or the way she said it. I mean, all that I really remember is dropping my glass and going after her with both hands. The rest gets kind of hazy.

We struggled a bit there on the sofa, I think that's a given. She kicked me, low and hard, right where it counted, but the rest plays out like an old home movie– the swing of my arm, her startled expression, my fist slamming into her face. I don't even remember the cops arriving or putting the cuffs on me. One of them may have given me a sucker punch to the back of the head, I can't be certain. I know that I spent the night in jail and the next morning, Stacy picked me up and drove me back to Hillcrest.

*****

"How's that?" Marion asks, giving her hands a rest.

I test my neck, moving it around, side to side, up and down. I don't mean to look at the clock, but I do anyway. I can't believe what time it is. I'm surprised I haven't seen the first gray light through the blinds yet. Pretty soon, the sun will be fully up and people will continue on with their lives. My brother said he would be coming in the morning, although, depending on how his night went, it could very well be much later than that.

"That's fine," I say. "Can you keep it up a bit more? If you can't, that's okay too, but it really feels good." I keep my eyes closed. These are magic fingers. I feel bad that Marion's been doing it this long, but I don't want her to stop. I'm afraid that the soreness will come back the way it has a habit of doing, especially when I think it's passed.

*****

When my mother died this June, it was only me and Marion at the funeral. A priest was there too, but he only said a few words, then hobbled away on his cane. It was a bleak day, unusual for the season. It was neither sunny, nor rainy; just gray, as gray as my mother looked when I last saw her. The whole ceremony took less than fifteen minutes. There wasn't a eulogy–what was there left to say? Afterward, we went to a Big Boy for coffee. My mother was dead and my brother had disappeared. I think Marion expected something more of a reaction from me. I wished I had one, but I didn't. All I felt was this sense of relief, like everything had been expelled. The gravedigger was polite enough to wait until our car had passed the site before he went about his work.

Kyle showed up in August. By this point, it had been well over a year since anyone had last heard from him. He had this way of popping in and out of people's lives like a malignant cancer. Just when you thought he was gone for good, he'd reappear at some inopportune time, when you least expected or wanted him. Maybe that's why I wasn't surprised when he pulled into the driveway that Saturday. Things were going good for me. I had been sober almost six months. I was starting to save a little money. Marion and I had started something. It might not have been as grand as what other people had, but it suited us fine. He pulled in, driving a Dodge Shadow, heavily dented in the front, no doubt the result of one of his drinking and driving escapades.

"Ray," he said to me, getting out of the car. "Guess who's back?" I almost didn't recognize him.

He was tan all over, wearing this loud Hawaiian shirt. He flashed me a big grin and spread his arms wide as if expecting someone to shower him with leis.

"Our mother's dead," I told him. He frowned. He didn't say anything for a few minutes. I don't know what I expected: A response, maybe anger, embarrassment, tears, anything. Instead, I got nothing. But this was Kyle, my younger, crazier brother. He just stood there looking at the brown spots in my lawn as if I had suddenly started speaking Russian and he didn't understand a word I said.

"Did you hear me? Our mother died. Your mother. We buried her, Marion and me."

"Damn," he said finally. Then he said it again, "Damn." He scratched the back of his head. He glanced back at the windshield of the Dodge. That's when I noticed someone else was in the car. The passenger door opened and this cute thing no older than nineteen–twenty, tops–stepped out. She had long, tan legs and straight, brown hair that curled toward her just above the shoulders. She was beaming. When she smiled, she showed a lot of teeth.

"Hi," she said. "I'm Sandy."

"Who's Sandy?" I looked at Kyle.

Kyle went over to the girl and kissed her on the lips. Not a quick peck, but a brief, intense make-out session. Then, with his arm around her shoulder, he turned to me.

"We're living together," he said. "That's what I wanted to tell you. I'm finally getting my life in order. I'm kicking the habit. I've come back home for good."

I didn't know what to make of this, so I invited them to dinner. Marion eyed me suspiciously, but what was I going to do? He was my brother and if he was serious about starting a new life, then the more power to him. He had as much right as any of us. We ate fast-food fried chicken and mashed potatoes that night and drank warm cans of Pepsi. Then, we all sat on the front porch and listened to Kyle relate the old days like he always did when we were together. He had a way of telling stories, something to do with pitch and pregnant pauses. Now and then, he asked me to fill in the details that he just couldn't remember. I did the best I could, but some of his blackouts are my own. Back in those days, memory was as long or as short as what was left in the bottle.

Marion just shook her head. She wasn't pleased. Before they left, Kyle and I shook hands and hugged; Sandy kissed me on both cheeks, the way Europeans do.

That should have been the end of it, but recently, two days ago to be exact, the call came in around one or two in the morning. It woke me out of a God-awful nightmare. I couldn't remember the dream exactly, but I was running from something or someone.

It was a child's nightmare, but it didn't make it less real, so when the phone rang, I was both relieved and frightened at the same time. It's not good when you leave one nightmare for another.

"Ray? Ray? That you?"

It took a little to adjust to the voice. It was one I hadn't heard in quite a while. It was drunk and heavy. I heard loud music in the background. Marion looked at me groggily.

"Who the hell is that at this hour?" she said.

That's when he spilled it: Sandy left him or he was leaving Sandy, whichever. The Great Experiment had failed. He was drowning himself at some bar and wanted to know if I would come out for a drink.

"I don't drink anymore," I told him evenly.

"Sure you don't, Ray. And my piss doesn't stink after eating asparagus either."

"Go to hell, Kyle." I was about to hang up when he broke down on the phone.

"I need help, Ray," he pleaded. "I'm gonna collapse. I need a place to stay. To recover."

I listened to him cry on the phone. In all of our years of drinking, I couldn't recall a single time when my brother had cried, even when his front teeth were shattered by a baseball bat. Marion kept watching me, looking for a sign, a signal. All I could picture was my brother weeping into some grungy pay phone someplace, where on the wall next to him, it promised that Susie gave head for a dollar if you called a certain number.

When I hung up the phone, Marion was right up in my face.

"He's drunk, isn't he? He is. I knew it. Goddamn, he's no good. I told you that, Ray. He's a bad seed. No good."

Something stopped her. I mean, I knew Marion. When she got started there was no slowing her down until she said what was on her mind, but I think she saw my face–the clenched teeth, the water in my eyes. The pain was that sudden. I tried to reach around and touch my spine. It was like an elephant was pulling at my muscles.

"What is it, Hon? What's wrong?"

The pain shot up again into my neck. I groaned. I tried to slowly lower myself back on the bed, but there was more pain: Shooting, sharp, intense.

"You're scaring me, Honey."

"My back," I said as my head hit the pillow. "I think I slept on it wrong."

\*\*\*\*\*

The last thing we need now is this, even if he is my flesh and blood.

I don't know how long we've been awake. It's been a while. Sunlight streams in through the blind slats. Long grill marks of illumination streak across the shag rug beside the bureau, and another patch equally long, by the bathroom door. Outside, I imagine it to be another beautiful October day, clear and crisp, weather associated with clarity and good judgment. The kind of day it hurts to take a lot of air into your lungs.

There's an image of my brother I have carried around with me much of my life, an image of the drunk on the day after, the torn shirt, the clotted blood, wreaking of a perfume of vomit, whiskey, and cigarettes. I picture him pulling into the driveway, half-packed and half-drunk, the only reminder of last night's free-for-all.

"If he were really serious about it, he'd go to Hillcrest for a while. I've known men like him all my life. Some can kick it and some can't, and Kyle definitely falls into the category of those that can't."

Marion's been talking, but I haven't been listening, not entirely. I fade in and out in sections.

We've been together long enough for me to know when I should grunt or nod my head. The truth is, I don't have to listen to know what she's saying.

"You've come so far, Ray. Why do you want to throw it all away now?"

"I'm not throwing anything away. I'm just giving him a place to stay and sort things out."

Marion stops rubbing. She stands and goes into the bathroom. She runs the faucet for a few seconds, and then walks out carrying a glass. She drinks some of the water, pausing to look at what's left. Something clicks in her head and she sets the glass on the night table as if it was poison.

"What if he drinks?"

She means, what if I drink. The thought has crossed my mind. My brother is a bad influence, there's no arguing that. He makes me remember things about myself that

I have long since buried. He represents a part of my life that I don't much like.

Since that last time at Hillcrest, there have been days when I can honestly say I haven't given booze a second thought. There have been days when I've been around the stuff, smelled it, and couldn't care one way or another. But then, there have been those other days too.

I stand and slowly stretch. The aches are still there, all in the right places. For someone who hasn't slept in God knows how long, I don't have that sluggish-sick feeling that accompanies lack of sleep.

When I was still drinking, I'd wake up with that feeling all the time. Sometimes it'd take a quart of orange juice and several cups of black coffee to make it go away. There were other cures, sure. People take all sorts of things, but that always worked best with me. One thing I've never quite gotten over is what a person will do to find remedies to keep on doing the thing that's causing the problems in the first place. We used to call it, finding the hair of the dog that bit you; not giving in to the hangover; not letting the booze beat you, not believing it could, even when it already had.

I look at the digital clock on the night table. It's ten past nine. I wonder if Kyle will show up this morning, today, any day. It wouldn't be the first time he hadn't done what he said he was going to do. My record isn't spotless either. Neither was our father's. He swore off liquor on several New Year's days only to find the bottle again. False starts are hereditary in my family, just like brown eyes and diabetes.

My heart skips a beat every time a car drives past the house. Like playing Russian Roulette, I think to myself. Sooner or later, the odds are going to get you.

"Ray? Are you listening to me?"

I turn to her. My mouth is open. I feel like I should say something, but I can't put words together.

Marion watches me, waiting, that look on her face. And then there it is: A noise outside, a car horn.

It goes off once, twice, three times. It's as if the person is firing away on the thing, purposely being as annoying as possible. I walk to the window and roll up the blind in time to see the black cherry Dodge weave into the driveway, battered and worn like an old boxer that refuses to go down.

"Oh, Jesus, there he is. What are we going to do?" Marion asks me.

Kyle gets out of the car, staggers a bit, and then puts a hand on the hood to steady himself. With his free hand, he rubs the back of his head. He's either got a killer hangover, or he's still drunk.

I turn briefly to look back at Marion. What can I tell her?

I walk out of the room and down the stairs. My feet are chilled in the draft and I suddenly remember that I've forgotten to put on my slippers. I read somewhere that the winters are supposed to come a little earlier each year on account of the hole in the ozone. Ozone or not, this town has been cold for as long as I can remember. I've grown up with this weather all my life. It's something I'm used to.

I hesitate as I reach for the front door. For the first time, I notice that my hands are shaking. My fingertips rattle against the brass knob.

Outside, Kyle rubs his face. He's half out of it.

I can see him through the window, crouching low to get his bearings. He looks like a quarterback drawing up plays in the sand.

"Ray?" my wife calls to me. She's standing at the top of the stairs. She bunches her robe together in front of her. There's that worried look on her face again, but she doesn't say anything else.

I use one hand to steady the other. It's a deliberate act, one that takes almost my full concentration. I grab the knob and turn it ever so slightly. Then, I open the door to help my brother.

## What's a Mother to Do?

My husband sits in the other room in front of the television. He remains motionless, staring blankly at the screen as if someone has sucked the life right out of him. Five days of stubble, marking every waking moment since this horrible ordeal first started, darken his face. His face is gaunt, the cheeks pulled in. I can't remember the last time he's eaten anything. I know I haven't, not in a long time. Looking at him now, he seems more like something made out of papier-mâché than flesh and blood–brittle, empty inside, rigid on the edges.

The local news is on. I can see the TV screen from where I sit smoking in the kitchen. A female reporter stands in the street right in front of our house.

She's a young thing, pretty, mid-twenties with a full mouth and brick-colored lipstick, very professional. Earlier in the day, she wanted to interview me or my husband about our son. Ideally, both of us, she said, but one would be fine. One would get the job done. She said that was where the real human interest angle was, in the parents. When you got down to brass tacks, that's what people really wanted to know about. "The story behind the story," those were her exact words. Ron wouldn't have it. He yelled at the woman, his face all flustered, jowls shaking like they do when blind rage has impaired his ability to speak, but she persisted, and when she touched his shoulder, well, that was the last straw. He just snapped, cursing her, using words like "bitch" and "cunt." Then, he shoved her back and slammed the door right in her face, without so much as a second thought.

"Goddamn reporters," he spat, "Why can't they leave well enough alone?" It was more of a plea than a question, something that doesn't require so much an answer as pity. Then, he marched back into the living room, taking his seat on the sofa, and stared at that blue TV screen. So, the woman and the cameraman taped the segment in the middle of the street. I watched them from the bathroom window. They seemed out of place standing there in front of our house which was almost paid for. Some of the neighbors came out to watch them. Ellie Morriss and Sy Renfeld were there, so were Lois Huber and old Mrs. Kadis. Their heads swiveled back and forth as if trying to match the reporter's

words with characteristics of the house itself–
broken shutters, cracked driveway, a lawn
sorely in need of mowing. They wore these
expressions on their faces like something
perverse was going on inside, as if complete
strangers suddenly lived there instead of their
friends, people they've broken bread with on
thousands of occasions. Ron must have seen it
too, because he shouted something obscene
out the living room window. His voice carried
and everyone looked on in horror.

Sy Renfeld, my husband's oldest
friend, just shook his head sadly.

The other night, certain persons–I'm
not naming names–vandalized our home.
There were four of them out there, distorted,
angry silhouettes hurling eggs at our house. I
listened to their soft cracks against the
windows, the staccato percussion that rained
intermittently like hail. Their yolks eased
down the panes in ocher smears. I don't have
to tell you that Ron had about had it. He
grabbed an old Louisville Slugger from the
front hall closet and stormed to the door.

"Don't go out there," I begged him.
"That's what they want you to do. Let's just
call the police, okay?"

"Sick of it," he said, his lip quivering.
"Sick of the calls, sick of the letters, sick of it
all."

"Ron."

There was this look in his eye. It frightened me. I withdrew my hand from his shirt. I withdrew my hand and bit my thumbnail. This wasn't my husband, this was someone else, someone full of anger, pushed to the limit; someone with nothing to lose. I wanted to cry.

Ron adjusted his grip the way a batter might do before stepping inside the box. But then, he did something else: He gently touched my arm. His fingers lingered there a moment before moving onto on my shoulder, easing me aside. Then, he threw open the front door.

"Get out of here! Get the hell off my lawn you miserable sons-a-bitches or there'll be trouble! So help me God there'll be trouble..."

He waved the bat menacingly and a slew of curses shot from his mouth.

Most of the instigators, whoever they were, took off, but not before they pelted him. They opened fire like some Hollywood parody of a gangster movie. Eggs sailed out of the darkness in a fury of white streaks, twenty to thirty peppering the front door and porch, exploding in patches of bright orange. Yolk spurted all over Ron's flannel shirt and jeans like large paint balls. A few caught him on the side of his head and in his face as well.

He let out a horrible scream and dropped the bat. He blocked his eyes with his hands. Then, the vandals took off. From the foyer window, I saw one last silhouette lingering on the front lawn. Maybe it was the way he was standing there, or the length of time, I don't know which. I don't know what he was doing, but I didn't like it. It was like he was watching my husband trying to gather himself, enjoying his suffering too much, sizing him up.

Something panged inside me. That's when I ran outside onto the porch.

"Go away!" I wailed. "You've done enough! Leave us alone!" I wrapped my robe around Ron's hunched form, shielding him with my body.

The silhouette hesitated. There was something in his hand I couldn't quite make out, but I'm sure he had something in his hand.

"Get inside, Gail," Ron said. When I didn't move, he said it again, "Gail."

I couldn't. How could I leave him out here? I watched the silhouette study us in the light–two fifty-somethings trying to make sense of all this mess; trying to contend with their guilt and what else? I waited for the stranger to do what he was going to do. Moments went by. I bit my lip. Tears rolled down my cheeks.

The shadow raised the thing in his hand then lowered it. "Perverts!" the voice yelled finally, then the figure turned and hauled off down the road.

I wanted to call the police. I wanted protection.

This wasn't right, even if, in some distorted way, it was understandable.

Ron said, "What do you think they were going to do? A couple of them were probably cops," he added.

He wiped his face off with his shirt-tail. There was a small cut beneath his left eye. Egg white dripped from his fingers.

"Goddammit," he said, heading toward the kitchen.

I looked out the front door into the night. Most of the nearby houses, especially the ones with small children, still had their flood lights on, burning accusingly at us in the darkness. Their bright hazes formed defensive perimeters around their properties, each one, its own protective compound.

The next day, I found a picture of our son, Michael, the one that's been in all the papers, tacked onto the front door with a pocket knife, the blade imbedded in his forehead. There was something written in red marker underneath it. It was one word:

*Molester!*

\*\*\*\*\*

Michael returned home to live with us after his second year in college. He hadn't flunked out, but he came awfully close. The state university put him on academic probation. They wanted him to take some time off to get his priorities in order. These things happened, they said. It was no big deal, but it had to be nipped in the bud before it got worse. I must say, this didn't come as a complete surprise to Ron or me.

Michael always had trouble with school. He had never been an "A" student and my husband and I both suspected from an early point that he would never amount to what you hope your son might in life. Only child or not, Ron stood firm: If Michael was going to live at home, he was going to live by his rules. There was no two ways about it. Ron wasn't going to tolerate weeknight partying or hanging out until unholy hours.

If Michael wanted to experience the real world, well, he was going to get his hands dirty.

\*\*\*\*\*

Michael tried his luck at a series of jobs– insurance, telemarketing, but ended up quitting or getting fired from each one shortly after being hired. Finally, as a favor to Ron, Phil Porter took him on his paint crew. They did all sorts of odd jobs, interior and exterior work, some light remodeling. To give credit where it's due, Michael was good at work he didn't have to think too much about, work where he could lose himself in the rhythm of steady physical labor. His effort showed progress, and it wasn't long before some of the neighbors hired Michael to do some things for them, off the books. Karen Brockman had him tile her bathroom. The Butlers wanted their spare bedroom repainted. George Carl added a small deck in back of his house. They weren't great jobs, but they added up.

They paid well enough to live on. I have to say, both Ron and I were grateful to our neighbors for that.

You always want better for your children. So he wasn't doctor or lawyer material, we didn't hold it against him. Sure, we want them to grow and learn and achieve more than we ever did. That's just the way things are. You always want yours to have it easier.

Children, God bless them, what's a mother to do?

*****

The one thing I can't help feeling is that this is all my fault. As a mother, you learn to suspend judgment over your child, no matter what he's done.

He breaks a window, cuts school. What can you do? You think there's nothing that a little more love won't cure, another kiss or hug, or, if all else fails, chocolate-chip cookies. After all, blood is still blood. Nothing changes that. It's what we all know deep down.

However, this whole incident has got me thinking. I'd be lying if I didn't at least admit that. I am doing more questioning than thinking, to tell the truth. I've spent the past few days going over everything from day one: Every detail, every reprimand, every decision, since we brought him home from the hospital, all eight pounds of him. When I think I have covered everything, I start all over again fresh, looking for more answers. Coming up empty is not a viable solution, you see. I spent all Tuesday sitting in the kitchen, reheating coffee, smoking and thinking.

It's not that the past is unclear, it's that most things I haven't let myself remember. Why would I want to? For instance, take this one incident in particular: Michael was in the ninth grade and I found his stash of dirty magazines in a shoebox in his bedroom closet. Growing up, all my brothers had them about the same age, so I wasn't completely taken for a loop. Boys will be boys, right? What never ceases to amaze me, though, is how they get them in the first place. There was a complex network involved, creativity and initiative, a certain bartering of goods: Bubblegum cards for firecrackers, a baseball glove for a Matchbox car set, a birthday gift you bought for him that he no longer used for something else.

The first two were run-of-the-mill dirty magazines, filled with typical shots of pretty, young, nude, smiling women and their centerfold questionnaires that disclosed their desires and dislikes, secret ambitions. I was fine with them, really. This was normal once you got past the initial shock of it all. But it was the last one that bothered me, the last one that buckled my knees and made me lean against the doorframe for support.

It was in a foreign language, German I think, and it showed several photos–disgusting photos–of young boys who couldn't have been more than eight or nine, engaged in various sexual acts with each other. There was one photo in particular, God forgive me, I'll never forget this, that had this blonde boy who was five if he was a day. His body was smooth and hairless, perfect in its innocence. What still haunts me is the face, the fear in the small, nervous eyes, the inability to understand, the revulsion. What's worse, the page was crusted over in what I could only think in horror was my son's dried semen.

I didn't know what to do. What can you do? What can anyone do? I remember crying in the kitchen, smoking in between bouts of hysterics. I stayed that way most of the day. A phase, that's what I kept telling myself, simple adolescent curiosity. What else could it have been? I wanted to confront him. I wanted to grab him by his shoulders and shake this out of him, whatever this was. I wanted him to feel what I was feeling. I wanted him to cry and be afraid.

But I didn't. I couldn't. I mean, how do you talk to your son about something like this? I made up my mind that I wasn't going to tell Ron. I couldn't bear to see his face. The disappointment would have been too much, especially after all the trips to the principal about Michael's grades. After all, Michael was still his only son, his one pride and joy.

When Michael finally came home that day, he went right upstairs. He stayed there a long time. I didn't want to think about what he was doing, but I couldn't help it. I pictured him on his bed, door closed, doing whatever, looking through that filth.

At dinner, Ron ranted on about the hardware store where he worked. He complained about Sy Renfeld, deliveries, the customers, all the while talking with his mouth full, stray bits of meatloaf spraying here and there. I didn't eat at all. I couldn't touch a thing. I watched Michael across the table, slowly chewing his food. He looked at me, his eyes questioning, trying to figure out mine. I looked away from him. Ron asked him about girls, and if he had any lookers in his class, any prospects on the horizon. Michael smiled shyly. He said he had his eye on someone and Ron let out a howl. He slapped his son on the back, tugging playfully on his nape.

"My boy," he said. "My boy's going to be a heart-breaker."

"Dad," Michael said.

Ron looked at Michael again and razzed up his hair. I felt like throwing up. I pushed myself from the table and went into the kitchen.

"Don't mind your mother," I heard Ron say. "You're growing up too fast for her. You know, women."

"Yeah, women," Michael said, and they both laughed again as if privy to the same secret.

*****

Outside two houses down, I watched Skip Olsen in his backyard. He was cooking chicken out on his grill. For some reason, I remember that succinctly– chicken–the scent of mesquite wafting in through the window screen. His wife, Marge, sat beside him, flipping through a magazine. From time to time she rocked a crib where their eight-month-old son, Ben, lay. They seemed so content doing nothing, just being one happy family. When Skip caught me staring, he turned to me and waved.

Nothing came out of it. From time to time when I knew he would be out of the house, I'd check his closet, but I never found another dirty magazine, women or the other. I don't know if somehow he knew I had seen them or not, but it stopped. I was grateful for that. I even watched him carefully over the next few weeks just to make sure, but there was nothing in his behavior to suggest anything deviant. I made myself get past it, happy I didn't make a big deal over nothing.

*****

A couple of years later–how could I forget?–I found Michael in the basement, snapping the heads off of crickets. He was with one of his friends, Doug Bernstein, a boy whom Michael had grown close to over the preceding summer. Doug was almost a foot taller than Michael was. He had stayed back a couple of times, a reading disorder or something like that, and he always wore this distant expression on his face, as if what he was looking at and what he was seeing were two different things. He set me ill at ease. Needless to say, I didn't approve of the friendship.

They didn't hear me come down the stairs. I saw them near the far wall, on their knees, hunched over, their backs to me.

"Check this out," Michael said. He had hit his growth spurt and his voice was mid-change. It was caught somewhere between teen and adult and sounded like he was speaking from deep inside a bottle. He moved his arm awkwardly, but I couldn't see what he did or why he had jerked it so suddenly.

"What's that green ooze?" Doug asked.

"Blood, I think."

"Gross."

Blood? Well, that did it. I raced down the remaining steps, my thick heels clomping. Michael whipped around, faced me. His eyes were panicked; his mouth formed a small "o."

"Mom!"

"What do you have there? What are you kids doing?"

Doug shoved something up inside his shirt. I couldn't see exactly what it was, but when he turned around the outline was unmistakable. More magazines, I figured, or something else.

"What do you have there, Douglas? Show it to me. Show me right now."

He just stared at me in that way of his. As I moved closer, he backed away, easing to my left. That's when I saw them on the floor. The small, dark bodies, headless, green ooze all over. There must have been twenty of them lying discarded, like used matchsticks. Near Michael's leg was a Maxwell House coffee can with air holes poked into the plastic lid. I froze in my tracks. My mouth was open, but I couldn't find my voice.

"Mom, it's not what you think."

If it wasn't that, what was it?

Ron talked to Michael. He told our son that his behavior was unacceptable. He told him a lot more things I'm sure. Then he removed his belt, the one with the large Budweiser buckle, and laid down the law.

When Ron climbed into bed later, he turned over on his side away from me. I should have seen it then. It had already started. A piece of Ron crumbled that night, just like that. I reached for him and touched his sweaty back.

"I don't want to talk about it," he said.

\*\*\*\*\*

I wish I could say it ended there, but this isn't that kind of story. There were other episodes as well, isolated incidents that have been reawakened by all of this. Panties disappearing from someone's clothesline, and public exposure on a bus. They were little things that had been completely erased from memory, glossed over by happier moments. Individually, they meant nothing, but when put together, painted a disturbing picture of my son.

Sergeant Harris paid me a visit shortly after three on Monday. Ron was at work. I was ironing shirts, watching my soap. I heard the doorbell and I swear, I wasn't going to answer it, but a woman knows when something's not right. The doorbell went off two more times and when I finally opened the door, Mel Harris was on the other side in his pressed blue uniform.

"Gail," he said.

"Yes?"

He didn't say anything at first. He chewed his lower lip. His eyes froze then looked down at the ground. His squad car was parked out front. There was another one too, in front of the Olsen's house, its lights flashing. There was an ambulance took to add to the confusion.

I got scared. Mel Harris did not stop by our house during the day ever.

"What is it Mel? Is it Ron? Is Ron okay?"

"Gail," he said again exhaling loudly, "we have a bit of a situation."

"Situation? What kind of situation? It's Ron, isn't it? My God, what's happened?"

"It's not about Ron, Gail. It's about Michael." He paused."It's not good."

They found Michael with little Ben Olsen in Olsen's house. He was doing some refurbishing in the basement, converting an empty concrete room into a play room for Olsen's son. I don't know the particulars. I don't want to know them, but little Ben came home from school. Then, a couple of hours later, Marge Olsen came home. I don't know how much time passed, ten minutes, an hour, but Marge went down the steps looking for Ben. That's when she found her boy with his pants down around his ankles and my son– give me strength–touching his privates.

I don't know. I used to think I was building my own fears with Michael, creating something out of nothing. I used to think that the real question was what more could I do, not where was my son going wrong? I used to believe that that was a parent's responsibility.

That's what they've been entrusted to do, but I'm not so sure anymore. I'm not sure of anything. I read somewhere that a child's behavior is a direct reflection of his upbringing, but that's not entirely true. This–whatever this is–didn't come from us. We never taught Michael this.

*****

Outside, the sky is dark. We've unplugged the phone. Too many calls, too many reporters wanting interviews or people telling us to go to hell, dark voices full of hatred, too familiar to be easily disguised.

The lawyer called earlier. Ron wouldn't talk to him. He just held the phone out to me, hand shaking, eyes pleading. The poor man is shattered, and who could blame him? This whole ordeal has taken its toll on him, on us. The lawyer wants us to take the stand, be character witnesses. He thinks it would be a good idea if we got up and told our side, paint the picture of Michael the public doesn't know, the ballgames, the picnics, the Christmas break pageants. There might not be enough for an acquittal, he said, but our son could get treatment. He could get help and that was just as good. That would keep him out of jail. Molesters didn't do well in jail, the lawyer said. "Trust me on that."

Thing is, when you get right down to it, I don't know if I want to testify. I don't know if I want to get up there before God, before everyone, and lie, even if he does have my blood running through him, even if we share the same color eyes and last name, even if he is my final product.

See, I've spent every, waking minute thinking about this. Lord knows, I wish I hadn't, but there it is anyway. Thinking about Michael, and Ben, and every other goddamn thing and the only question I have, the one that keeps escaping me, is why. Why? And when I can't come up with an answer, no reasonable explanation that would bring some sense of clarity to it all, I suddenly become frightened.

And you want to know why?

It's not that I fear for his well-being, or wonder where I went wrong as a parent, or if he's mentally sick, or anything like that. I wish I could say it's because I'm concerned about Ben and the Olsens and everyone else affected by this incident, but that's not true either, even though I'm sorry that it happened. I'm sorry that any child has to experience a debasement such as what my son has caused. The simple truth of the matter is that I want Michael to die for what he's done. It's not the sanest thing, I know, but there it is. I don't want his lies, his problems, or his disappointments.

I don't want him anymore.

When is it, if ever, all right for a mother to stop loving her son?

*****

Ron hasn't said much to me. I wish he would. I wish he'd get out what he's feeling. We need to talk it out between us, to accept it all, the guilt, everything.

How can we move forward, if we can't come to terms with what's holding us back?

Someone parks a car in our driveway. I hear its door slam shut and then the clicking of leather soles against the macadam. I imagine what type of shoes they are, wingtips, maybe, or loafers, something hard, and forceful, and polished.

The doorbell rings, a loud, dull noise. It's a familiar sound by now, one I've heard a thousand times inside of five days. It goes off again.

"Don't answer it," Ron says. I look at him, waiting for him to meet my eyes, but he doesn't. He doesn't move at all. It's like he's paralyzed.

I finish my cigarette, grinding it out in an already full ashtray. That's when I notice my fingers shaking. Not bad, but shaking nonetheless. It's as if they have a will all their own. I regard them a moment, twitching nervously, and when I can't make them stop,

I use one hand to steady the other.

Over the past couple of days, I've been in the habit of checking the peephole, asking for a name before opening the door, something you might teach a child to do. Guilt works that way. It's an awful lot like fear. It's something that passes between people. It's silly, I know, but there it is anyway.

I mean, after all, what is there to be afraid of? Who could it be on other side, am I right?

*****

I open the door and let in the smell of fall, of dying leaves and crisp, cool air. For a moment, I don't move. I breathe in deeply a couple of times, the fresh oxygen stabbing my lungs. The neighborhood looks almost normal again.

The figure before me is silhouetted in the afternoon light. He is a large man, wide at the shoulders. There is something in his hands.

"Who is it, Gail?" Ron calls out from inside the house. His voice is so strained and edgy I almost don't even recognize it. "Gail?"

I raise a hand to shield my eyes from the glare of the late sun. It's the lawyer; I'm sure, wanting to go over the case with us. He had mentioned something earlier about affidavits and releasing a formal statement. He's been through unsavory business like this before. He's good that way. He wants us to be prepared for the long road ahead.

Part of me wouldn't be surprised if it was someone else either: Not a reporter or a policeman, mind you, but someone entirely different, like that man the other night–Skip Olsen even–preparing to deliver us from all this shame.

"What is it, Gail? Who's at the door?"

What is there to tell? We just stand this way, me and this dark man, not saying a word. It's as if we've come to an agreement on something. Then I smile and lower my hand from my eyes, opening the door a little wider.

"Hello," I say, "We've been expecting you."

## Complete Absence

I sit on the hood of my car smoking. It's humid out, late August. The sun's going down, bleeding everything orange and red. It's a glorious sunset, but I'm not thinking about that: I'm thinking about how much I could use a beer right now.

But I can't. I mean, I'm on the wagon. I've promised my brother, George, I've given him my word. If you know me, you know that that doesn't count for much. I've given my word plenty of times before and not kept it. I'm not proud of this fact, but it's the way things are.

Across the street, my brother's neighbor eyes me suspiciously. He doesn't recognize me and he shouldn't. I just got into town about ten days ago.

He's an older man, not used to seeing strangers, I'm sure. He sets up his sprinkler on the front lawn and, every so often, casts a nervous glance my way.

Yesterday, I tried to be friendly and waved at him, but he just stared right through me, as if he was worried I was going to rob him blind the moment he turned his back.

I inhale deeply, allowing the smoke to gradually sift from my mouth. My brother doesn't like me lighting up inside his place, so I have to smoke outside. He doesn't like me smoking at all, but some things you have control over and some things you don't.

When I pulled up in front of his house, he and his wife, Jill, were pacing the front stoop like a pair of concerned parents whose son still hadn't made it home from the prom.

I hadn't seen him in over a year and the first thing out of his mouth was, "We don't allow smoke inside the house, Mikey," as if it made me less of a person because I smoked.

But I can't complain. I mean, here he is, letting me stay at his place rent-free, until I can find my feet again. So what the hell? Smoke outside? It's the least I can do. I'm not so much of a bastard that I don't appreciate a generous act.

When I was living with my girl—ex-girl—Janine, we'd light up wherever. We lived over a garage then. It was a one bedroom apartment, but it had a ragged economy to it—a half-fridge we kept stocked with beer, a stove with two burners, even a little black and white TV with rabbit ears.

This art teacher she knew at the local high school let us have it for practically nothing. It was cramped at times and had a sloped ceiling on one side that I'd bang my head into when I was drunk, but it suited us fine. We had ashtrays all over the place, on window sills, the bathroom, one on each side of the bed. We also drank a lot, no question, but smoking was, by far, our biggest vice. For a stretch, there were few saving graces in that relationship, but smoking and drinking were two of them.

But I'm here to find myself, not rehash the past--that's what my brother said, and he's right. I have to make sense of things, get back on track. He had no trouble putting me up, but I have to do some serious soul-searching. I couldn't keep on the way I was going, he said.

He made me promise that I'd use this time to fish around for answers, come up with a plan. No booze either, he also said that. He wants me to cut down on the cigarettes too, but first things first.

*****

This morning, George and Jill left for a long weekend in the country. They had been planning on this for a while, long before I busted in on their routine. I walked them to the car, opened the trunk, and placed their bags inside. Then, my brother turned to me and said, "You going to be all right?" He sounded concerned, but what he was really concerned about was the liquor cabinet upstairs.

It was another beautiful day, and we were standing out front. Cars zipped by. George's neighbor, the old man, was down on his knees digging in his flowerbeds. He looked back at us from time to time and dragged one gloved hand across his sweaty forehead.

"Fine," I said aloud. "Five days and counting, the hard part's over." I managed a weak smile and tried a joke. "Who knows better than me, right?"

He shuffled his feet. "You're too old for me to watch over, Mikey. Like Mom. If you want this, I mean really want this, this is the right step. No one can force you. You've got to want it."

Jill touched my shoulder the way women do sometimes. "He'll be fine, George. He doesn't need any more sermons. He knows, don't you, Mike?"

I nodded.

"See? He knows, Honey."

Jill's a good girl. I've met her twice before– once, five years ago at Thanksgiving, the other, at my mother's funeral. She's got a good heart. She's someone who always believes the best in people. She has the patience of Job, especially where my brother's concerned. For that, she deserves a medal. She's put up with a lot of shenanigans, not just his, but my own too.

I wasn't on my best behavior during Thanksgiving dinner that year. Everyone drank wine with dinner. I had straight bourbon. I can't remember how it started, but an argument broke out and things just escalated from there. I said some things that night–unkind things. I wasn't in my right mind. I sent my mother to the kitchen in tears.

George dragged me out of the family room, my arms flailing. That's the kind of brother I am: The first time he brings his girlfriend home, I go and do something like that. I never apologized for the embarrassment he must have felt, although I've wanted to several times. It's a futile moment in my life, one in a long string of them, too far removed to serve any purpose.

It was George's turn to look at me. He stared hard at my cigarette and bit his lip.

Jill threw her arms around my neck and kissed my cheek. Jill's a real beauty. She's part Filipino and part Chinese, which gives her this dark, exotic look.

She's someone you'd look twice at if you passed her in the street. My brother could have done a lot worse. Lord knows, I have.

"Don't make me regret this," he said.

I shook my head and smiled. I dropped my butt on the ground and squashed it. Then, I offered him my hand as a show of good faith.

He looked at it a minute, then brought his own hand to his chin and rubbed. When he finally arrived at some decision, he took my hand and shook once, hard and firm, like our father taught us to do.

\*\*\*\*\*

The other day–Wednesday, I believe–I found myself calling Janine. I was in a bad way. I woke with the shakes and was scared. George doesn't understand the shakes, but Janine does. We hadn't talked since the morning after her birthday party, the morning I cleared out for good, bruises and all. She badgered me every step of the way that day, poking me with a finger, getting in my face.

"Worthless!" she shouted over and over, each time louder than the last. "Worthless!"

Worthless? I wanted to remind her that only one of us had a job. I don't think I saw a carton of milk paid for by her artistic expression. It seemed to translate into everything but money. That was the type of artist she was.

There are things that happen between people that can never be taken back, and just as well. I said some things I'd been meaning to say, but didn't get to say all of them. My head was reeling and my tongue was slow. If I had stuck around, it would have turned ugly. I would have killed her or she would have killed me. On my way out, I shoved the last bottle of Old Crow off the table and watched the sticky brown fluid splatter and spread across the cheap linoleum.

"Get out!" she screamed, "Go on! Get out of here! Get the hell out! I hope you twist your car around a tree, you drunk bastard!" She tried to stand in my way to yell at me some more, but I didn't stop for anything.

I pushed right past her and went out the door. I made it down the steps to my car before she came after me, throwing an old baseball that barely missed my head and dented the driver's side door. She stood at the top of the steps, her old, unwashed nightgown open, breasts exposed, throwing things and shouting obscenities as I backed down the driveway.

Strange thing is I'd be lying if I said I didn't miss her, and I don't want to lie anymore. That's in the past for me. Fact is,

I'm sorry about what happened, for the things I'd done, and for the person I was. Don't get me wrong, there were good times too, little things that I remember, like the fact I used to call her "Baby" when we weren't fighting.

"Baby," I'd say, "Baby, you hungry? You want me to fix you something to eat?" Or "Let me massage those shoulders, Baby, you're so tense." Each time, I'd kiss the inside of her palm and she'd know I'd mean it. It seemed to make a difference.

My fingers shook as I punched in the numbers. My heart felt like it was going to come out my chest. The phone rang and rang. I had nothing planned out. I didn't know what I was going to say to her even if she picked up. What's left between two people when everything crashes into a dead end? The answering machine kicked in and I just stood there breathing into the receiver, hanging up before the beep.

She should have been home, but she wasn't. In hindsight, maybe it was better that way.

*****

I fish around for another cigarette. I'm smoking too much now, even I recognize that. I tried chewing gum for a couple of days, but stopped when I couldn't find a flavor I liked. I'm very particular about what I chew–no peppermint, no spearmint, no bubblegum. Cinnamon's okay, but not too much of it. And the nicotine gum? Don't even go there.

You'd think the same would hold true for my cigarettes, but fact is, I'll smoke any brand. When I used to date the girl before Janine, Claire something-or-other, I smoked whatever she smoked. When we first met, we smoked two different kinds, but eventually I bought the same 100's because it made things easier. I mean, it was less hassle at the convenience store. Eventually, we'd end up buying a carton and just helping ourselves.

Janine was the exception though. She smoked these thin jobs, with barely enough tobacco for three hits. I tried them, but they didn't take. They were absolutely horrible– thin and feminine. I got my share of looks smoking those. Now, I buy whatever I see first–Winstons, Camels, Marlboros–it doesn't matter, as long as it keeps my hands busy.

My hands are still shaking. I try holding one out in front to see if I can keep it steady, but it doesn't work. It trembles, and no matter how hard I concentrate, I can't make it stop. I can't even light my cigarette, that's how bad it is. I've been through the shakes before. It's something that happens when you're drying out.

The first time I tried to kick it, Claire (or was it Carol?) took me to her parents' cabin upstate. There wasn't a lick of alcohol to be found, nothing that even hinted of the stuff, no maraschino cherry juice, not even vanilla extract. I shook something fierce then, a week of them. I couldn't even feed myself, Claire had to spoon soup into my mouth like I was some sort of paraplegic. I sweated a lot too, but that came later.

I've done my best to hide it from George and Jill. They shouldn't have to spoil their plans on my account. But Christ, what I wouldn't do for a little something to calm these down. You hope to hell you bypass the shakes, but you never can. They stick with you a while, a reminder of what always could happen.

I've seen people go into seizures before because of them. One moment, they're talking to you, and the next, they're down on the floor, eyes rolled back, convulsing. A doctor told me once that it had something to do with the shock to the system, to the complete absence of alcohol. It's like hitting rock bottom going ninety with no brakes.

It scares the hell out of me. My body has taken its share of booze, and here I am almost two weeks without a drink. I was fine up until a couple of days ago, but then they started. I hadn't even thought about drinking, but this morning I woke up with a thirst for the stuff, which means I'm officially "clean," and going through withdrawal. The DT's, shakes, whatever you want to call them, are back and they frighten me every time.

*****

Janine used to say I was desperate. Desperate and crazy, that was my problem, she said. I was like a pinwheel spinning and crashing with the wind. Who knows, maybe I was. Sure, there were nights when I'd drink a fifth of bourbon then strip down naked and run outside with my arms over my head, screaming at the top of my lungs. I was always doing crazy stuff like that.

But for every good moment there were twice as many bad ones. My brother said it first–two people cannot careen out of control and expect to come out of it without some damage. Something had to give. One night, a year into my relationship with Janine, he tracked me down by phone. He had heard some things, he said. People he knew–our friends–had seen me one night leaving a bar, and it hadn't been pretty. I don't remember the night in question, but I'd heard stories about it. Janine and I drank too much and got into a shouting match. Outside, we caused a disturbance and the police came. She hit me a few times before they took us away. The next morning, we paid our fines and headed right to the liquor store for another bottle. That was my life with Janine: Filling up then crashing, then starting all over again.

Not too long after, everything seemed to have dried up between us. I don't know if I'd go so far as to call it love. What is love anyway? Whatever it was, the affinity that once existed had definitely disappeared.

We just didn't care anymore; I can thank the booze for that. That's when you know you've reached the end, when you're indifferent to seeing the pain you cause in the eyes of the one you're supposed to love.

Then, on her thirtieth birthday, she threw herself a party. She invited all of her friends–burn-outs, greasers, lowlifes of every shape and form. Her paintings, abstract portraits and dizzying colorful montages, hung on every inch of wall space. Even the unfinished stuff, the "works in progress" as she liked to call them, were stacked neatly in a corner, a shredded tarp barely covering the dingy canvasses.

People milled about, sipping wine out of fat, plastic glasses. I was already drunk by the time most of the guests arrived. They talked in know-it-all voices and admired her "eye" and perspective. Someone threw in a John Coltrane tape on the boom box. These people talked of art and writing. They complimented each other. This was supposed to be a big deal, some high affair. It was a load of crap.

Later in the evening, around three or so, I could barely stand. Everyone was lit. Some were making out on the couch. Two women danced and touched each other right in the middle of the kitchenette.

Janine was cornered by the art teacher and from where I was standing, she didn't look like she minded one bit. He had one hand on his drink and the other around her waist. He leaned in close when he talked. She French-inhaled her smoke.

And then, I don't know, something came over me, a temporary moment of blindness, or maybe the shit had finally been piled too high. I jumped up on the card table. I almost broke my neck doing it, but I stood up there and dropped my pants in front of everybody. Some looked, some didn't care. Most of her friends kept on doing whatever they were doing. They had seen this or worse from me before.

"Get down, Michael, you're making an ass of yourself." Janine tried to sound like she wasn't worried, but she knew better. She knew I was crazy, that I could do anything at a moment's notice.

"Art? You call this shit art? I'll give you art. I'll give you all the art you can handle." I grabbed my penis. I shook it in front of her art teacher friend. "You like art? How do you like this?" I hosed down the front of one her paintings.

All hell broke loose then. I ripped another of her masterpieces with a corkscrew before someone stopped me–the art teacher maybe? I don't know. My arms were pinned behind me. I might have even been punched a couple of times, I don't remember.

The next day, I woke up with bruises all over my face. Janine had thrown most of my things outside already. I got up and put on my pants. My head was splitting. She shouted obscenities at me every step of the way, but I didn't care. There's no reconciliation for people in that frame of mind. No hope for it either.

*****

I smell my fingers. They say when you've stopped smoking, you can smell traces of it on your fingers. Everything smells foul and pungent, your clothes, your room, your hair. It makes you wonder why you even started smoking in the first place. It must be true, because I can't smell a damn thing on mine. I smell and smell but there's nothing, just skin.

Booze doesn't work like that. Booze is a different animal all together. You feel it all the time. Your heart goes all crazy, jumping up and down, when you know it's near. A reformed smoker can turn his back on cigarettes, but not a drinker. An alcoholic is only a step away from his next drink.

I can't help but feel empty inside, and in a strange way, I am. I'm in my own body, jittery, but alcohol-free. This is a new and profound experience for me, and it's scary. I'm all alone and there are four bottles of wine and a fifth of Jack upstairs without a lock.

I recall what my brother said to me at our mother's funeral. It was some time ago, long after he moved four states away to escape whatever it was he was running from. It didn't make much of an impression on me then, but for some reason, I remember it now.

We were standing by the grave. The priest and the friends who had attended had long since disappeared. Jill was waiting in the car. She hadn't said much to me, but she had smiled and been polite. I saw her ring. They had been married a year then. Imagine my brother being married a year and I hadn't even known about it to send him a card.

I offered him some of my flask, but he shook his head. I drank anyway and he watched me swallow.

I didn't know what to say. We hadn't talked much since he pulled out. There wasn't anything to talk about. George shoved his hands in his pockets and looked at the ground.

"So, Mikey," he said. "What happens now?"

I smiled. I always smiled when somebody said something to which I had no response. I shrugged, drank some more. Then, he did something he hadn't done since we were kids. He put an arm around me. He put his arm around me and talked in my ear, real low, so low that it made me feel uncomfortable.

"Take a good look, Mikey," he said and nodded to our mother's coffin. "That woman wasted so much of her life. Think about it. She ended her life at thirty even though we buried her at fifty-five. She just took the roundabout way of getting there. Drinking? Shit, a piece of rope would have been quicker."

He clenched his fist and jaw, then shook his head. He looked back to the car and shrugged his shoulders. It was late afternoon, I was drunk and my mother was dead. I finished the flask and watched the smoke leave my lips and disappear over the six foot hole in the ground.

"You see what I'm saying, Mike?"

*****

It's darker now, midnight blue. The old man's sprinkler still swishes back and forth, and for a moment, I'm tempted to run through it like I used to do as a kid.

George will be back in two days. Two days. If I can just hold on that long, I'll be okay. I'll make it. But two days is an eternity for someone like me. Two days is a lot of time to be filled. I have my cigarettes and that's fine for now, but what about later? It's later I'm worried about.

I know it's hot and muggy, but I'm shivering just the same. My skin is rough with goosebumps and sweat beads my upper lip. I wonder if Janine ever felt this way, ever allowed herself to come down, cleanse her system. I wonder if my mother did either, or if she ever gave herself a chance to.

After I finish this last smoke, I'm going inside and run a bath, let the steam rise and fill the room. It's crazy I know. Who else would be thinking of a hot bath right in the middle of all this heat, but I am. I haven't taken a bath in years but it's on my mind now: Slipping into that water and resting my head against the tile, closing my eyes for a spell, see what happens from there.

It's a filthy habit, smoking. I'm quitting soon, I have to. I have half a mind to call Janine again and tell her to quit. I'll ring her in a few days after the shakes leave, or maybe I'll do it now. Now is just as good, I mean, if not now, when? I want to tell her some other things first. I want to apologize. I want her to know how sorry I am for everything. I'll want to cry, but I won't.

Sure, she'll be surprised when she hears from me, that's a given, but maybe we'll get to talking after the initial unpleasantness. Maybe, we'll find a thread, remember what it was we had together. She'll invite me over for a drink, which I'll decline of course. I'm sober now, I'll say, I've got no more room for drinking. She'll make a comment and probably sit back on the sofa near the table and light a cigarette. I'll hear the flint strike and the hiss of flame as she brings it to her mouth. She'll inhale and pause a moment, all rage and despair.

"What do you want, Michael?" she'll say finally, exhaling, the blue smoke leaving in a jet from her lips, disappearing somewhere in that hollow, empty room.

I'll smile a bit and my mouth will quiver. I'll bring my hand to my face and wipe the sweat off my lip. I'll shake all over.

"What is it, Michael?"

I imagine sitting across from her. She's in her nightgown. Her hand is pressed against the table, her fingers spread wide. She'll look at me funny when I lean toward her, bringing her hand to my face like I used to do. I'll remove the cigarette from her trembling fingers. My voice will go soft. That's when I'll tell her.

"Baby," I'll say in such a way, she'll know that I mean it. Then, kissing the inside of her palm, I'll put the cigarette out.

## Rain

My wife sits next to me in the passenger seat, staring out her window. Farmland slides by barns larger than half-city blocks and silos like skyscrapers shooting up toward the sky.

The more I see, the more I think this is a good way to live, the right way to live–in an old house surrounded by wide open spaces and fences. Nothing is able to get in or out without you seeing it cross the fields, or hearing it in the uneasy squeak of the front gate. Whether or not she sees what I see, I can't be certain. How can you know what goes on inside another person's mind? My wife remains silent as if concentrating on the pictures in her head instead of what the scenery presents. She has barely moved an inch in two hours if you don't count bringing a cigarette to her lips every ten seconds. Between her fingers rests the last cigarette of a carton she's finished in the past two days. I take one hand off the wheel and squeeze her thigh. She offers me a smile. It's fragile, like blown glass, something that can easily be chipped or broken. From the way her eyes glisten, I know she's trying, and that's all that matters. I bring her free hand to my mouth and kiss the soft interior. A little further, I tell her. Just a few more miles and then we'll be there. She nods and keeps her vigil out the window.

We've been driving God knows how long. It feels good to be back behind the wheel, going on a trip somewhere, just the two of us. The last time we did something like this was when we borrowed my buddy Jim's cabin upstate to celebrate our one year anniversary. It was a little place that overlooked a small man-made lake that the state stocked with trout at the beginning of every fishing season. It wasn't fishing season then, but we had a fine time just the same. You couldn't ask for a better view. The leaves were just changing. We brought some groceries, cheese and crackers and a few bottles of wine that she refused to drink. We read on the porch and took long walks through the woods. We had some things to talk over. She wanted to know how I felt about having a kid, but I wasn't ready. Then, one night over a dinner of canned stew, she sprung it on me: She was expecting. I nearly flipped out. You're mad, she said. I was but I wasn't, not really. The whole thing took me by surprise. She tried to tell me that it wasn't an end, but a beginning. A beginning to what, I asked her. She got up and walked away from the table. I went outside. That was only three years ago, but it seems almost like another lifetime, before all this other stuff happened.

The doctors agreed a trip would be good for her, to help alleviate some of the stress, they said. The guilt would work itself out in time, but for now, the mental stress from the accident was eating away at her worse than any cancer. There was little more they could do for her. If she was going to snap out of it, she was going to have to do it herself. I didn't watch our son die right before my eyes, so I haven't pushed her to get better. The mere thought of his little body smashing through the windshield is enough to make me vomit.

\*\*\*\*\*

After another mile or so, we start seeing the first signs for the inn. I ask my wife if she is cold and when she doesn't respond, I ask her a second time. She slowly shakes her head once or twice in a way that makes me wonder if she understood me at all.

Her mother didn't want her coming on this trip so soon after the accident. We talked about it Monday over at my house. She was running a load in the dishwasher.

"It's too soon," she kept saying. "She's not ready for this."

What did she think I was doing this for? If therapy was actually getting anywhere, it'd be a different story, but three times a week, I watched my wife sit in a chair in a blank room and not even acknowledge the therapist in front of her. She spent each two hour session just staring straight ahead, oblivious to anything and anyone save for whatever shadows her mind had locked on.

After the last session, the therapist told me that one day she was just going to wake up. "I've seen these cases before," she said. "They don't respond to anything and then one day, it's like they just open their eyes and are back in the land of the living. There's no rhyme or reason for it, it just happens."

I wasn't satisfied with that, so when I proposed to her mother that I take her away, that's when all hell broke loose.

"You have to be patient with these things. You take her away now, there's no telling what might happen!"

I told her I had to do something. I just couldn't sit and wait. Then, we got into a fight. She screamed some things at me. On her way out of my house, she was shaking her head, but my mind was made up. I had to do something. The next day, I made some phone calls, and when the woman on the other end asked for my credit card, I gave her my Visa number.

*****

We pull off onto a dirt road that weaves us to the inn just as the last orange light disappears from the sky. The gravel driveway crunches softly beneath our tires like popcorn or those plastic packing bubbles kids love to snap. The inn looks inviting from the front, a large wrap-around porch complete with swing and rockers, something right out of The Waltons or any of those idyllic fantasy-land dramas where mortgage payments magically appeared, and children pulled through terminal illnesses. I park between two other cars in front, a Volvo and a Ford, with license plates from Massachusetts and Michigan. I smile at my wife, who sits there unfazed, the smoke curling from her filter. Even the cracks and paint chips ooze the tranquility of a different lifestyle than we are accustomed to. It's just as it was promised, quaint and private.

*****

I carry the bags and check us in. The woman behind the desk is all smiles. She's old with perfect blue-white hair and a small mole above her lip. She's dressed in a gray cardigan with holes in both elbows and a long, pleated wool skirt. She asks me questions that I answer with a nod or shake. She's been in the business long enough to know when people want to talk, and when they just want a hot shower and sleep. She accepts my abruptness with a cordial patience and hands me the room key. She releases a large, brass ring into my palm.

Two old men study a chessboard near the spit and cackle of a fire. They are dressed in red and black flannel and look more like they're from these parts rather than visitors from out of town. Both look at me as I pass by. One spits tobacco into a tin cup and nods a hello in my direction. The other drinks a tall glass of milk. I watch his Adam's Apple as he swallows, and, when he's finished, he too gives me a curt nod as if he's confirmed something. I take my wife's hand and lead her up the stairs. I cannot help but feel this is the right move for us. Even the boards have a pleasant groan in them as we walk. I tell her this, but she's gone off into that other place she occupies when she's not with me. It's like this sometimes: One moment here, the next, somewhere I can't reach her.

*****

In the morning, the warm smell of coffee percolating is enough to entice me from sleep. I glance over at my wife who's breathing lightly on her side. She's had a restless night and it's a relief to see her calm and relaxed as if she's actually enjoying her dreams instead of always running from them. I slip out from beneath the sheets, pull on a fresh pair of jeans and an old work shirt speckled with paint, and step quietly out the door.

Downstairs in the dining room, there is one other couple besides myself. They're both around ten years older than me, mid-forties or thereabout. They're familiar enough with each other to sit and read sections of the local paper while they eat. They switch when they're finished, and, except for the briefest of smiles, they don't say a word, content to share the occasional glance or two. I sit down at a small table and wait to be recognized. A few moments pass before the old woman from the night before glides by.

"Right with you in a sec', Dear," she says, whisking what smells like a basket of bran muffins and a pot of hot coffee over to the couple.

She breezes back over with astonishing dexterity for someone whose age I figure to be around seventy. She places a hand on her hip as she stands in front of me. Nothing, it appears, slows this woman down.

"What can I get you this morning? There's coffee, tea, juice, freshly-baked muffins, toast, waffles, or eggs made to order. And if you're the adventurous sort, I can whip up some of my world famous scrambled eggs, made with a little bit of cream cheese for extra fluffiness."

She adds a smile after fluffiness. It's obvious she is someone who prides herself on her kitchen.

"Coffee would be great for starters, and I'll take a muffin or two if it's no trouble."

"No trouble at all, Dear," she sings and disappears behind swinging doors. When she returns, she wields a small carafe of coffee and a basket full of bran.

"Try some apple butter on them, Sweetie," she says, producing a small porcelain jar from her apron and handing it to me. "Just made it yesterday, don't you know."

She waits to see if I do what I'm told. I do. I split a steaming muffin and smear a generous portion of the butter on top and pop it into my mouth. It's delicious as promised and I wash it down with a sip of coffee that burns my tongue.

"If you're a sweetheart, I'll let you in on the recipe before you leave. But only if you are a sweetheart." She winks to let me know that she's kidding.

My mouth-full, I nod my head. Her eyes dart from the empty seat back to me.

"The missus sleeping in today?" she asks. I can tell by her tone that this is a friendly question and not a nosy one. She is someone who is used to knowing things about her guests. It's her way of making a connection with the hundreds of faces that wind up at her front door, looking for something they can't find at home.

"Yes. Yes, she is," I reply, adding my own smile to it. Over the past month, I've grown accustomed to answering questions about my wife with a smile. It's become habit, part lie and part defense mechanism. Truth is, I don't know how my wife is feeling or doing most of the time. I sure as hell wish I did, but I don't. "The ride took a lot out of her I'm afraid. She hasn't been feeling well lately."

"I'm sorry to hear that. But after a nice, relaxing weekend, she'll be a hundred percent, I'm sure. Believe me, no one comes here sick that doesn't walk out of here with a clean bill of health. You'll see. If you want, I can whip her up some of my world famous Hannifan Soup. Secret recipe's been in the family for years." She smiles politely.

"That would be great," I tell her. Next to being the nicest person in the world, this woman must be one hell of a cook. Everything is world famous with her.

She quickly scans the room, stopping first at the couple, then moving, checking for any sign of movement in the front hall. When she seems satisfied that no other guests have risen yet, she seems to relax. She sighs loudly.

"Where are you all from?" she asks. "That is, if you don't mind me asking. I kind of like to get a feel of where my guests come from. It's nice that way. Once, someone made the trip all the way from Arizona, can you believe that? Tombstone or Tucson, I can never remember which. But you don't have to answer if you don't want to. I don't want to pry where I'm not wanted."

Her face has this lonely quality about it, something old, and tragic, and wonderful. To not answer would not only be rude, but almost an insult, like telling your wife's mother to shut the hell up and mind her own business.

"Just outside the city," I say biting into another muffin. "We came down for a little break. I guess we both needed to get away. High stress lifestyle."

The woman starts to wipe down a table that already has a tarnished glow. The more I stare at her, the more I realize that she is, in fact, a lot like my wife's mother–always seeing something that could be done.

"I don't blame you. Can't stand the city myself, too many damned cars for one thing. People get down on the smokers, but I tell you it's the exhaust from those contraptions that's going to be the death of us all."

She lifts her head and smiles at me to make sure I'm not offended.

"You have a point there," I answer, raising the mug carefully to my lips. Slowly, my body responds to the caffeine. It's a good feeling, one of re-awakening and power.

"Now, take Horatio for instance. He smoked a pack and a half of Chesterfields a day and lived to be seventy. Now that's something." She suddenly turns to look at me. "Horatio was my husband."

"Oh." I make a mental note: Was.

She snaps the rag once and furiously wipes down the back of a chair now. Out of the corner of my eye, I see the couple preparing to leave. I guess they've both had their fill of small town hospitality. I am unsure if you're supposed to leave a tip in a place like this and hope they will provide me some kind of clue.

Her hand disappears inside one of the sweater pockets and removes a pack of cigarettes. She looks at me briefly before taking one out.

"You smoke?" she asks suddenly.

"No. No, I don't. I quit about a year ago. But my wife still does. She quit too, but started back recently."

She nods, then lights up. She takes two quick puffs before grinding out the cigarette in a nearby ashtray.

"Got to take 'em when I can get 'em," she says.

I help myself to another muffin.

\*\*\*\*\*

That night at the lake house, I stayed outside long after my wife went to bed. I was still smoking then and I smoked a pack of cigarettes listening to the silence of the woods. It hadn't rained in a while, but it looked like it was going to. Someone told me once that when you were out in the sticks, there were two ways you could tell it was going to rain: If the night sky was covered in a gray haze, and if you couldn't hear even one damn cricket chirping among all those trees and tall grass.

I stayed out there when the rumbling started. It came from the mountains and moved down steadily toward us. The rain came shortly afterward, breaking into a sudden downpour. I listened to the heavy sound it made on the fallen leaves. I walked off the porch, stared up at the sky, and let that cold rain splash down all over my face. It poured so hard I couldn't even open my eyes. And then I did something else–I ran. I ran as fast as I could. I ran like someone possessed, like someone with everything and nothing to lose. Even when I fell, head–first, I picked myself up and kept running while the rain fell all around me.

*****

The older couple walks out as a new couple enters. They select a table not too far from the kitchen. The woman glances shyly over at me and smiles. The man says nothing. They sit down. Their eyes are bloodshot, puffy. They have that look about them–as if they were up the whole night arguing. I know that look. He drums his fingers on the table while the woman adjusts the silverware around her. I notice that his finger has a wedding ring around it and hers doesn't.

"This is place is so cute," she says. "Don't you think it's cute?"

"It's fine," says the man. He scans the room, pretending to look at things. He scratches the stubble on his cheek.

The old woman bursts through the door.

"Morning!"

She goes over to their table and takes their order. Then she buzzes back through the swinging doors. For a while, the couple doesn't say anything. He looks at some of the framed prints of ducks on the walls. She rubs the area around her ring finger.

"You could at least try," she says.

"I am trying, Ei'. I'm here, aren't I? If I didn't want to try, I certainly wouldn't be here, that's for damn sure."

"Don't do me any favors."

"Don't get started. This was your idea, remember."

"Our idea. This was our idea. I want to make this work."

"It is working. Things were going fine."

"Things were not going fine, Vern. You–" She stops when the old woman brings out their food. They, too, have chosen muffins and coffee. The old woman smiles and dips into her apron. She removes a small jar of apple butter and leaves it, then hurries off to bus the other table.

"She's sweet, that woman. Did you know she runs this place herself? I mean, she has two guys help her with the food and stuff, but she pretty much runs this ship alone." The woman splits a muffin and smears some butter on it, but she doesn't eat it.

"What happened to her husband?" Vern asks.

"Died, I think. Same with the son. They may have died together, I'm not sure."

"That's uplifting," he says.

"I heard it from Marjorie. She's the one that told me about this place. She came here with Donald when they were having problems."

"For crying out loud, we don't have problems! I just made a mistake and it's over!"

She ignores him as she watches the old lady reorganize a table.

"Would you look at her? She's got such strength. God, I wish I had her strength. Then nothing would affect me."

"Eileen," he says, softening. "You don't mean that."

"Like hell I don't."

She looks as if she's going to say something else, but puts a finger on her lips instead. "So, Vern, what are we going to do?"

*****

When I first saw my wife in the hospital that night, she was curled in bed like a cat, the sheets drawn up tight around her chin. She was rigid as if bracing herself for some attack she could anticipate, but couldn't locate. Astonishingly, she hadn't been hurt. In fact, there were no stitches or broken bones, nothing to suggest she had been involved in that horrible twist of metal and broken glass, but a few minor scratches on her cheek. I guess I was a bit shocked, expecting something else entirely. A one in a million chance, the doctor told me later, nothing short of a God-given miracle. But she couldn't or wouldn't respond to my presence at all, wouldn't even to blink when I waved my hand in front of her eyes. He assured me that that was normal for someone who had been through what she had. He even had a word for it–catatonic–complete withdrawal. Then, as a matter of comfort or recourse, he put a hand on my shoulder and added that my son hadn't felt a thing.

I sat in the orange chair across from her bed. There was some duct tape on the cushion and some old magazines on the table beside it. I watched her all night as she stared blankly into the mute emptiness of the hospital room. I could just imagine what her senses were reliving, the whine of the brakes or the glass shards pelting her face like a hard rain the dark image of a two-year–old boy suddenly disappearing from view.

*****

The old woman comes out with a fresh batch of coffee. She goes around refilling cups, first mine, then Vern's and Eileen's.

"Let me warm those up for you," she says to me, scooping up the bran muffins and carrying them into the kitchen. She pops through seconds later with a fresh rag in her hand. "Out in a second," she says and attacks the table with a renewed vigor.

There is something about this woman I can't put my finger on. She is full of this nervous, bustling energy, the kind that is not so much impressive as it is troubling.

Vern and Eileen are still talking, lower now. I can't quite make out their words so much as read their faces. Whatever it is, it's not going well. They're making too many gestures. They haven't even thought about their food. The muffins remain piled in the basket like lumps of brown coal and suddenly, I feel embarrassed for our hostess.

The old woman senses something too. When she glances at the couple, her expression shows concern. That's when I notice that her eyes have the faint swirl of approaching cataracts. White shadows curl around each lens, giving her a smoky, sad quality, the kind that makes you want to throw your arms around her and squeeze for all you're worth.

When Vern and Eileen feel like they're being watched, the old woman returns to rubbing down a chair. She hums something unfamiliar to me. Her voice cracks in places although it's a nice melody, almost a lullaby. I turn to the window and wonder if my wife is still asleep or if she is sitting on the bed with her knees drawn up, staring at the wall.

\*\*\*\*\*

The official report went down as an accident. An eyewitness said he saw the blue pick-up weave past his car over the yellow line and collide head first into my wife's Honda. Another said he was drunk or crazy or else had just fallen asleep at the wheel. In any case, my two-year-old son was dead. The funny thing is, I'm sure I knew what his reaction was when he saw the two unfamiliar headlights bobbing toward him, bright and unimposing, like the Christmas lights on our tree. I can just picture him raising a finger at the windshield and looking toward his mother smiling.

"Hot," he would have said happily before the impact.

\*\*\*\*\*

It's overcast outside. The sky is covered with long, steel-gray clouds. A wind picks up from time to time and stirs the trees. Neither Vern nor Eileen has spoken for some time.

The old woman stands by the front door. She looks out the window like she knows what to expect, like she can sense something coming just by the way the air feels or smells. She holds a cigarette in between her gnarled fingers. She inhales, taking her time releasing the smoke from her mouth.

"Look at her," Vern says. "What do you think drives a woman like that?"

Eileen fidgets with a cold muffin. She has already broken the top into pieces and is now picking at the bottom half.

"What do you mean?"

"She runs this place herself, isn't that what you told me?"

"So?"

"And she probably ran this place before. Am I right? Before everything happened to her."

"Yes. I guess so. So what?"

"So, everything changed, everything that she knew, everything that she held dear. It hurt, I'm sure. It hurt like hell, but she didn't give up. She could have, but she didn't."

"Vern."

"No, I'm serious. Hear me out. For no reason whatsoever, this woman woke up to find everything different. But she dealt with it. I mean, it probably affected her in some way, but she got past it. You said so yourself–she's got strength. But what kind of strength? The kind that gets you past things."

"Vern, that's not the point."

"But it is; it is the point. It's exactly the point. You say we have problems, but what problems could we have compared to her? Compared to anybody? We make our own heavens and hells. Do you see what I'm saying?"

Eileen doesn't say anything right away. She takes several minutes to digest what's been said. She watches the old woman by the front door. She watches as she brings the cigarette to her lips, and watches her fingers tremble when she pulls it away.

When she looks like she has decided something, she reaches across the table for Vern's hand. They touch and her fingers rub his ring. They stay that way for a few moments, neither one saying anything as if some understood agreement has been reached.

The old woman walks back into the room. "It's going to rain today," she says matter-of-fact. "Hope you all brought your slickers."

\*\*\*\*\*

When the rain ended, there was a chill in the air. It hurt to breathe. I was soaked right down to my socks. I walked around the lake and looked at things. Down by the water, I even skipped a few stones. The noises returned slowly–insects, animals–gradually venturing out after the storm. It was like everything was waking up for the first time.

I had an impulse to run hard and fast, I remember that. On the way back, it hit me: I didn't want that kid. I wished to God that it was all a bad dream. I even imagined that I would go back to the cabin and she'd be waiting for me at the door and say, "April Fool's" or something, and then we'd both have a good laugh and maybe screw the rest of the night.

But when I got back inside, I saw my wife's sleeping form wrapped tightly under those blankets, and in that moment, I knew that things were never going to be the same. I went over to her and stroked her hair, combing it with my fingers the way she liked so much.

She stirred sleepily, fluttered her eyes and smiled when she saw me. She nuzzled my hand and in a voice not fully awake said something to me.

"Daddy," she said.

*****

The old woman hands me the basket with the piping hot muffins. "Thought I forgot, didn't you?" She laughs. "Careful, they're hot."

She watches as I split one and spread a healthy dose of apple butter on the insides. The aroma is unlike anything I've smelled before. She nods contentedly as I shove a half into my mouth and chew quickly.

"That's it," she says happily. "That's the way to eat 'em. Spread it on thick."

She examines me as I eat and, for the first time, I notice how tired her eyes look beneath their buoyant exterior, how the skin sags like the skin of an old peach. I wonder how many nights this woman has cried when no one else was around.

Vern and Eileen have already left. They walked out hand in hand, leaving their breakfast untouched, that segment of their lives forever unfinished. The old woman snaps her rag to attention, bussing the table and wiping it down. Cleaning is a job that is never quite done to her satisfaction.

Another couple makes it down stairs. They're young, no more than twenty-four, twenty-five tops. They smile at each other. The boy nervously presses his girlfriend to go in first. The old woman excuses herself and sees to their breakfast. It seems they have good appetites this morning. She brings them a pot of coffee, eggs, and the homemade bran muffins. In between her trips, the boy kisses the girl twice; once on her hand, and once on her cheek. The girl smiles both times.

The old woman has a strange expression on her face, as if caught in some kind of intimacy. She busily makes everything clean again. Her hand moves back and forth, picking up speed, then slowing down, then fast again. I wonder what thoughts a woman like this has.

"Better be careful if you're headed outside," she says to anyone who's listening.

The young couple says nothing. I finish my coffee.

Upstairs, my wife still sleeps. She is curled into a loose fetal position with the blankets brought up tight around her shoulders. Her face is almost an angel's, but I can tell there is too much agitation in the dark circles beneath her eyes to be any real peace there.

The rain comes down harder than I've ever heard in my life, harder even than at that time at the lake. I open the windows wide to let in some of the fresh air, but then close it a little. I think of how good it would be for her to go outside and run around, to let all that cold rain wash over her body and wake her from this state. But this is a woman who can barely walk on her own, much less run.

I watch her a while and listen to the troubled sound she makes when she exhales. Then I strip off my clothes and lie beside her, throwing an arm over her waist, molding my body against the soft contour of hers. I catch the rhythm of her sleep and breathe when she breathes.

*****

I am very much afraid.

## Meet our Author
## Emilio Iasiello

Emilio Iasiello is the author of Chasing the Green (FEP International, 2008). His short fiction and poetry have appeared in numerous academic and literary journals—Buffalo Spree Magazine, The Larcom Review, Oasis, Krater Quarterly, New York Review, Iron Horse Literary Review, The California Quarterly, The Washington Review, and The Wilshire Review, as well as many others.

An avid screenwriter, he has optioned several screenplays, three of which have been produced into films: Saint Christopher (2002), P.J. (2008), and Chasing the Green (2009). Chasing the Green won the Award for Excellence in Filmmaking at the 2010 Canada International Film Festival and the Best Supporting Actress in a Feature Film Award at the 2009 Los Angeles Action on Film International Film Festival. P.J. received the Best Actress Award in the 2008 Miami Underground Film Festival. Dead of Knight was completed in 2010.

A devotee of the theatre, Emilio has had his stage plays produced in Baltimore, MD; Washington, D.C.; Los Angeles, CA; New York, NY; and London, UK.